Where There's a Duke, There's a Way

Dukes in Danger
Book 7

Emily E K Murdoch

ARE YOU SIGNED UP FOR DRAGONBLADE'S BLOG?

You'll get the latest news and information on exclusive giveaways, exclusive excerpts, coming releases, sales, free books, cover reveals and more.

Check out our complete list of authors, too!

No spam, no junk. That's a promise!

Sign Up Here

www.dragonbladepublishing.com

Dearest Reader;

Thank you for your support of a small press. At Dragonblade Publishing, we strive to bring you the highest quality Historical Romance from some of the best authors in the business. Without your support, there is no 'us', so we sincerely hope you adore these stories and find some new favorite authors along the way.

Happy Reading!

CEO, Dragonblade Publishing

Additional Dragonblade books by Author Emily E K Murdoch

Dukes in Danger Series
Don't Judge a Duke by His Cover (Book 1)
Strike While the Duke is Hot (Book 2)
The Duke is Mightier than the Sword (Book 3)
A Duke in Time Saves Nine (Book 4)
Every Duke Has His Price (Book 5)
Put Your Best Duke Forward (Book 6)
Where There's a Duke, There's a Way (Book 7)

Twelve Days of Christmas
Twelve Drummers Drumming
Eleven Pipers Piping
Ten Lords a Leaping
Nine Ladies Dancing
Eight Maids a Milking
Seven Swans a Swimming
Six Geese a Laying
Five Gold Rings
Four Calling Birds
Three French Hens
Two Turtle Doves
A Partridge in a Pear Tree

The De Petras Saga
The Misplaced Husband (Book 1)
The Impoverished Dowry (Book 2)
The Contrary Debutante (Book 3)
The Determined Mistress (Book 4)
The Convenient Engagement (Book 5)

CHAPTER ONE

4 February, 1811

ARTHUR HEBBLETHWAITE, ERSTWHILE Duke of Fitzpaine, tried to smile.

"Ah," he said helplessly. "Snails. Wonderful."

He had been a fool not to expect it. He was in France, after all, and snails were supposed to be a delicacy, weren't they?

He had never understood it himself. If you wanted to eat something slimy, there were plenty of hearty English foods that fit the bill. A pork pie. A hearty fish stew. A roast chicken with the grease still dripping from the haunch.

Why the poor Frenchies had to descend to something found in an English garden . . .

But that wasn't the point. Right now, he had to put aside his intense dislike of the horrible slimy things and work out which fork he was supposed to use to eat them.

He assumed fork. Arthur had never eaten snails before. Perhaps it was a spoon? A delicate knife, designed to winkle the things out? He'd had winkles before, delicious little things, but those had been eaten from a paper bag while swinging his legs over a seafront wall. Nothing like this.

"Ah, my good Duke of Fitzpaine," the French captain said

with a magnanimous grin. "I am disappointed to say we do not have the proper utensils for escargot. We will have to make do."

Captain Blanchet carefully picked up a fork.

Relief swam through Arthur's chest. "Ah, yes. Such a shame."

"We dishonor ourselves in front of you, the great duke from England," continued Captain Blanchet. "We shall have to hope as you continue your stay with us, we can impress."

Arthur forced more debonair arrogance into his expression. "Yes, you will."

Gritting his teeth and hoping the dozen or so French captains around the table had not noticed his absolute desire not to eat the slimy things—*still in their shells!*—Arthur leaned forward, picked up the fork, and started to prize one out.

It was a good thing this was the first course. Arthur was certain if he'd already eaten, he would be seeing a repeat of his food. Still, he hadn't come all this way to be unmasked merely because of a snail.

He popped the slimy thing in his mouth. Thankfully the cook, whoever they were, had coated the things with so much garlic, it was impossible to know what it tasted like.

Arthur forced himself to swallow. "Delightful," he said, eyes watering.

There were murmurs of approval around the long table and soon every man was heartily eating.

It was the perfect distraction. Carefully not breaking eye contact with the man opposite him—Arthur had already forgotten his name—he slipped a snail off his plate and onto the floor. The dog which had been sniffing around since they sat at the table quickly scooped it up.

Arthur tried not to smile as he heard the crunch. The dog appeared half starved. At least someone would appreciate the snails.

His gaze flickered about the room. It was the sort of place he'd expected. The large manor the French regiment had requestioned had an impressive dining room, walls covered in landscapes and a beautiful chandelier above. The room was packed with captains, colonels, and there was apparently even a major somewhere down the table.

There were also, as Arthur had expected, women. Most of them looked thrilled to be here, dining with the dashing French captains they evidently idolized.

There was a war on, after all. And you couldn't have a war without heroes.

One, however, looked terrified. *Plucked out of a local brothel and brought here to entertain,* Arthur thought privately. Her blonde hair was finely dressed, but her eyes sparkled with fear.

A pity he could do nothing about it, even if she was seated to his right. He'd had no opportunity to speak with her and his attention was immediately taken again.

"What an honor it is to have you with us, Your Grace," Captain Blanchet, seated to Arthur's left, was saying. "I had no idea the Duke of Fitzpaine was even in France!"

Murmured conversations muttered around the room. Arthur smiled nobly and leaned back in his chair, effortlessly at ease.

He had quickly ingratiated himself with the captain thanks to his impressive title. *The Duke of Fitzpaine.* It did indeed sound mightily striking.

Such a shame it was a complete lie.

"Oh, I had not intended to be in France," Arthur said, completely honest for once, as he pushed his hand through his hair.

One of the ladies farther down the table met his eye and shot him a covetous look.

Arthur managed to avoid it. Oh, she was pretty, but he couldn't allow himself to get distracted. Not yet. There would be plenty of time for dalliances with beautiful women when he had truly convinced these idiots he was a duke.

Him! A duke!

It was laughable. Certainly anyone who knew him in England would have considered it ridiculous.

But here in France, there were no rules about things like that.

No way to prove who he was—or any way to disprove it.

And so he had traveled the place under the assumed name and received great welcomes wherever he went. Dukes were always welcome.

"Why did you come to France, then? In the middle of a war?"

The question was asked by a lieutenant several seats away. Arthur could not recall his name. In truth, he could not recall if he had ever been told the man's name. There were so many of them, nearly twenty in all, and only one of him.

Besides, the wine in the glass in his hand was remarkably good. What was it about French wine that stole all memory from you?

"France in war is still France," Arthur said, spreading his arms wide impressively.

There were nods and laughter around the room.

A strange shiver rushed up Arthur's spine. As he had spread out his hands, he had gently grazed the arm of the poor woman beside him. The one in the blue gown, who evidently did not wish to be here.

Arthur's jaw tightened as he glanced at her, preparing an apology in his best French.

The woman was looking studiously away, as though she could pretend he was not there if she looked away long enough.

Arthur shrugged, putting her out of his mind. He wasn't here to *rescue* her, after all. Not that she needed rescuing. *Any woman foolish enough to work in a brothel during a war*, he thought darkly, *knew what she was getting into*. Even if she did not like it.

No, he didn't want to get into any sort of entanglement. That wasn't his way. Arthur Hebblethwaite did not get ensnared by women.

Especially not ladies of the night.

"And how are you finding France, now you are here?" Captain Blanchet said with a wide grin. "I suppose it is a disappointment to you that the English are losing so spectacularly."

There were roars of laughter, fists banging on the table, feet stamping. The whole cacophony was deafening, and Arthur forced himself to smile through it.

The blackguards. They had no idea how the war was going, and neither did he. No letters were getting through the lines at the moment, which suggested there was heavy fighting.

But of course, he couldn't just speak his mind. That would never do.

When a man is pretending to be a duke, you had to nod and agree, in part, with everyone. At the end of the day, they would then be forced to agree with you. You were the duke.

Arthur grinned. *It was all rather fun.*

"I suppose so," he said airily. "Though I will admit, the fact I am walking about around France suggests there is not much in the way of security."

The lieutenant glared. "Just because the captain permits you to—"

"Permits me?" Arthur said, attempting for his most haughty. *How was it he had sounded in Paris? Ah, yes.* "You think anyone *permits* the Duke of Fitzpaine to do anything?"

It wasn't until he raised an imperious eyebrow that the young lieutenant looked away, but he did look away.

Arthur congratulated himself silently on a job well done.

It was a wonder real dukes didn't run the world, he could not help but think. As soon as anyone found out—or rather, as soon as he told someone he was a duke—they couldn't stop themselves fawning, bowing, scraping. Anything he wanted, anything he needed was provided.

No wonder dukes were so happy all the time, he thought bitterly. If he'd had this all his life, he'd have no problems at all. Everything would be perfect. *Instead . . .*

Well, he was a duke now. There was no reason to return to his life in England, no reason to reveal the truth of his birth or the fact that the dukedom of Fitzpaine did not even exist. He could live the life of luxury here in France for the rest of his days, war or no war.

"And what will you do when we win?" The lieutenant's face was red now, verging to purple. "When all the English have been thrown from our shores and—"

"Maurice!" barked Captain Blanchet. "Mind your manners!"

Arthur saw with relish that the young lieutenant rose in anger, pushed his chair back without saying a word, and stormed from the room. The door slammed behind him.

Thank goodness. If that had continued much longer, he would have to think of a way to have the man thrown out, and that was remarkably difficult, even for a duke. Particularly an English duke in France.

"I do apologize, Your Grace," said Captain Blanchet, servility dripping from every word. "The man has no manners, and he has never been in the company of such refinement."

Arthur sat a little straighter in his chair. "Not at all."

"I take personal responsibility and do hope you'll see your way to forgiving—"

"Yes, yes," Arthur said carelessly, waving a hand. "I am of a forgiving nature, my man. All the Fitzpaines are."

Why did it give him such a thrill to speak in such a conceited way? And why, Arthur wondered, did it give him even more enjoyment to see the way people reacted to such rudeness? The more arrogant he was—the more outspoken, the more directly rude—the happier and more polite other people seemed to become. It was the strangest thing.

And it played right into his hands.

"Ah, the next course," said Captain Blanchet, looking up with glee. "I hope you enjoy bouillabaisse, Your Grace?"

Perhaps he did. Perhaps he didn't. Arthur was in no position to answer either way, because he had absolutely no idea what the dish was.

"Of course," he said boldly, leaning back again in his chair. It was one of the tricks he had noticed years ago. Gentlemen, real gentlemen, always leaned back in their chairs. The more relaxed they were, the higher up the echelons they appeared to be. "Though naturally, I doubt whether your concoction can compare to that of my French chef back in London."

It was perhaps too bold, but not many heard him. The room was growing warm, candles lit throughout, cigar smoke starting to blossom to the ceiling—the entire proceedings were raucous. A few of the ladies had found themselves, most happily, in the laps of the captains. The only woman who had not appeared to have made a gentleman friend was the silent blonde beside him.

Arthur glanced at her.

There was something different about her, something that appeared more and more enticing the more he looked. But he could not put his finger on it, not without considering her for a great deal of time.

She was elegantly beautiful. Perhaps that was it. The other women were clear in their intentions, eager to gain the protection of a man in the French army, but not this woman. She assiduously avoided the gaze of every man in the room. She had barely touched her food. There was a tautness and a tension in her shoulders—

"Well I hope we are able to impress, even if your French chef is as good as you say," said Captain Blanchet genially. "Ah, here we are."

Serving men continued to enter. Arthur was unsure whether they were soldiers, forced to serve their betters, or if the captains kept servants for such a thing. Either way, most averted their gazes from those at the table as they placed bowls before each man.

Arthur looked down. Within what appeared to be river water swam a great deal of undistinguishable slimy things in the bowl.

Of course. What was it with French cooking?

Oh, they may call it cuisine, but Arthur wasn't fooled. It was just an excuse to get rid of all the little pests and mites in one's gardens and ponds, he thought with a wry smile. The smile was forced away rapidly, though, in case it was spotted.

He had managed to remain in France as "the Duke of Fitzpaine" for months now, and he was enjoying himself. It would never do to lose his cover so swiftly. The title of duke would get you everywhere.

And so it was with a great deal of bravado that Arthur looked into the face of the man who placed his bowl of disgusting stew before him.

"Thank you, my man," he said brazenly.

And froze.

Oh, hell. That had been a mistake.

A light of recognition, far off but growing, appeared in the man's eyes. "My pleasure, Your . . . Your . . ."

Arthur's jaw tightened and he tried not to show even an iota of panic in his eyes.

What were the chances? Here he was, hundreds of miles from London, perhaps a couple of hundred miles from where he was born. He'd come all this way for a better life, and when he had been unable to earn one, he had merely slipped on the false title of Duke of Fitzpaine like another man would put on a coat.

It had served him well for months. Very well, truth be told.

Which was why it was so unfair he was about to lose it all.

"Don't I know you, Your Grace?" said the Frenchman slowly.

The French captain was quick to snort—quicker than Arthur was able to think. "Know the Duke of Fitzpaine? Oh, I don't think so, Laurent! I would consider that most unlike—"

"No, I am certain we have met before," said Laurent, his eyes narrowed on Arthur.

Arthur attempted to look nonchalant as his gaze flickered around the room.

Only the one exit. He should have thought of that before he entered this damned place. The door was far along the other side of the wall. He would have to pass at least ten Frenchmen before he reached it.

If he reached it.

"The Duke of Fitzpaine is our honored guest, and I did not

invite you to speak to him," Captain Blanchet was hissing just within Arthur's earshot. "I did not ask your opinion—"

Arthur's heart was pattering in his chest. But he'd been in worse scrapes than this, hadn't he? He'd always managed to come out of them with his skin. Mostly.

"—but I tell you, sir, that man cannot be the Duke of Fitzpaine—"

Arthur gave his best attempt at a dry laugh. "Goodness me, that is the first time that my parentage has been questioned!"

There were red spots in Captain Blanchet's cheeks. "I am most sorry, Your Grace, I do not know what is wrong with the man! I will have him flogged—"

"No need for that," Arthur said hastily.

Hell's bells. He didn't wish to be unmasked as a fraud, but that didn't mean he wanted a man to suffer the agonies of a flogging. Damn, he should never have accepted this particular invitation. He had been on his way elsewhere and his ego had been flattered, that was all. If he'd kept on his journey, he would have been miles away by now.

"I tell you, that is not the Duke of Fitzpaine!" the servant was saying as he was marched toward the door by another servant, the attention of every officer at the table now firmly fixed on Arthur and the unfolding spectacle. "That's—Arthur! Arthur Hebblethwaite, is that you?"

Only then did Arthur remember.

Christ alive, how was a memory from five years ago so difficult to recall? Yet it was only as the man called his name, his true name, that the face rushed back to him.

It had been cold. Arthur had been working as a lackey, a man of all works, at an inn just outside London. There had been a Frenchman there staying with his master. There had been no other place for the servant to sleep and so Arthur had been forced to step aside and give his own bed in the stable to the brute.

He'd not thanked Arthur. Of course he hadn't.

Now he was thanking him even less.

"You're just a man, a servant, you're no duke!" Laurent yelled across the table, wrenching himself from the other man's grip. "He's a fraud!"

The silence could have been cut with a knife.

Arthur was tempted to do just that. He had a knife tucked into his belt for just such an occasion, though he had never been forced to use it. Not until now. He'd never been in such a dire situation as this.

And that was perhaps why he did something absolutely idiotic.

Rising to his feet in a sudden lurch, Arthur grabbed the wrist of the woman in the blue gown. He pulled her, unprotestingly, to her feet, and yanked her before him.

And then he raised the knife.

"No one move!" Arthur yelled into the shocked silence. "I warn you!"

He did not need to spell out precisely what he was warning. The knife at the woman's side said enough.

A few captains rose to their feet slowly, their chairs falling behind them, but one look at Arthur's face made them slowly resume their seats.

His breath was quick and the woman in his arms was shivering—*with fear no doubt*, he thought. Well, this hadn't been his intention. He had not considered the beauty as a hostage until the very last moment, and even then, he felt wretched doing it.

But she was his only guarantee of escape.

"No one follow me," Arthur growled, slowly moving around the table to the door.

The woman in his arms did not resist. She walked with him—*almost*, he found himself thinking, *as though she wished to be gone from there also.*

When he was in the corridor, movement from the room echoed through the open doorway, but Arthur heard Captain Blanchet bellow, "Not yet! He still has her!"

That's right, Arthur thought as he increased his pace, pulling the woman through the labyrinthian corridors toward the back door. *I have her. My own guarantee of escape. For now.*

The back door flung open and Arthur saw several soldiers look round in surprise. He slipped the knife back into his belt.

"The lady and I require a horse," he said sternly.

Again, the "knowledge" that he was the Duke of Fitzpaine made him far more persuasive than bribes or threats. Within moments, a horse was brought forward.

"Get on," Arthur muttered to the woman.

For a moment—just a moment—she caught his gaze.

Arthur's lungs tightened. Such a look. Fear. And anger.

And then he was mounting the horse beside her, kicking his ankles into its sides, yelling, "Yah!"

As the horse careered from a standing start to a gallop, Arthur saw from the corner of his eye the officers pour out of the back door. One of them had a gun and he fired it, missing the fleeing horse.

Arthur started to laugh as they cantered out into the dark, following the road and aiming for the lights in the distance.

He had done it! He may not have finished the meal—a small mercy—but he had retained his life. And he was still the Duke of Fitzpaine.

After about ten minutes, Arthur slowed the horse to a trot, his heart still hammering. Then his attention turned to the woman in his arms on the steed.

Ah. Right.

"Mademoiselle," he began awkwardly. "I—what the—"

Startling him, the woman slipped from the horse's back, tumbling from his clutches. Arthur pulled the horse to a sudden stop and mirrored her, staring in confusion.

Where did she think she was going?

Well, he would just have to try his best French. Clearing his throat, Arthur began, *"S'il vous plaît, pardonnez-moi—"*

The woman glowered and shot back in refined English. "How dare you!"

CHAPTER TWO

JOANNA'S LEGS WERE shaking but she wasn't about to let this brute see that.

Trying to hold herself as stiffly as possible, as though she had been treated the last two weeks as the lady she was, Joanna tried to meet the brigand's eye.

"*S'il vous plaît, pardonnez-moi—*"

"*How dare you!*"

Her voice shook a little more than she had wished, but she was astonished she could speak at all.

It had been a nightmare for days and somehow she had stopped caring what was going on around her. She had barely noticed the bold and brash gentleman beside her at the dining table. Her attention had been on the food, and the panic in her chest, and the hatred in her lungs for every single one of them there.

They must have known, mustn't they, how she came to be there?

So it had been almost as much a surprise to her as the rest of the table when this brute, whoever he was, had grabbed her and threatened her with a knife!

Her! Joanna Bettencourt!

Well, he was going to feel mighty foolish when he realized just what he had done, Joanna thought, panic sparking through her lungs.

And she would have said as much. If she weren't so much of a coward.

"How dare I?" the man repeated. "You . . . you are English?"

Joanna tried to hold the man's gaze but there was such intensity there, it was quite impossible. He seemed to bore through her eyes into her very soul. It was difficult to know how to look at him, a challenge to even to think.

And she was tired. Everything in her ached.

The nightmare had begun weeks ago, perhaps even a month. It was hard to tell. What day was it?

"You are an Englishwoman?" the man repeated, taking a step toward her.

Joanna hastily took a step backward, lifting her hands to ward him off. "Stay back!"

"But—God's teeth, I had never expected . . ."

The man's voice drifted away as he examined her more closely.

Joanna felt the flush rising up her neck and across her cheeks. She had always hated being looked at, always hated being pointed out as the shy one.

At least now, in the darkness of the night, she would not have to suffer the indignity of having her embarrassment be so obvious.

Her legs were still shaking. How had it come to this? What did this man want with her? Would he hurt her?

He certainly would, Joanna reminded herself. *He was willing to threaten you with a knife to escape. He would do anything to keep himself safe, even hurt you. Remember that.*

Perhaps he had already happened to another woman. There was that Lady Genevieve Cotton-Powell, wasn't there? No one had seen the sister of the Earl of Armstrong for years.

Could this be what had happened to her?

"I do not appreciate being used as a hostage," Joanna said curtly.

It was a relief, in truth, to speak English again. French had never come naturally, and though she could get by, when a native speaker spoke, it was swiftly a struggle to keep up.

Not that she was about to admit as much to the man before her. *Cad!*

Joanna shivered. And she was all alone with him, in the middle of the French countryside, with no money, no way home, no pelisse—

"You're cold."

Her shyness prevented Joanna from actually looking at the blackguard as she replied, her words harsh as her anger at being used rose. "Of course I'm cold. It's January."

"It's February," the man said flatly.

Joanna's gaze met his, just for a moment, then she dropped it to look at her hands.

February? Was it possible it had been so long?

Well, she had hardly been aware of some of the days passing into night. The weather had been so awful for a time, it had been hard to know what was night and what was just gloom.

So, it was February. Were they looking for her? Did they assume she could never be found?

"What do you want with me?" Joanna whispered to her hands.

Panic was spreading through her chest, making her skin prickle with anticipation.

She knew what gentlemen like this did to ladies they found in the middle of nowhere. Unprotected. With no name, no brother, no father to protect them. No husband . . .

Joanna tried to swallow but her mouth was dry and her throat scratched. So this was how it was to end. She had thought one of the French captains would eventually try something but they had been remarkably polite and civil.

Unlike this brute.

"But—you are English! I don't understand."

Despite her fear, Joanna forced herself to look up. "*You* are English."

He was more than English. He was remarkably handsome.

Joanna could not force away the thought, but then, she would not share it either. And it was the truth.

The man, whoever he was, was tall. Taller than she had thought when he had been seated. He was wearing the impressive clothes of a gentleman, even if he did not act like one. His long hair was dark brown, though Joanna was vaguely aware it may have shimmered into black in the candlelight, back in the manor. She had not really been paying attention. His jawline was sharp, just a hint of beard appearing on his lips, chin, and cheeks. There was a haughty expression in those eyes that she knew well.

That of a gentleman.

"Th-That servant," Joanna said, her shivers quivering her speech. "H-He said—"

"Here, take this."

She shied away the moment the man took a step. "Stay back!"

Fear was not an unknown companion and Joanna had thought she had learned to live with it weeks ago. Months ago, if this truly was February. But this man had such power, he exuded so much authority. She knew, if he wanted to take her, there was nothing she could do to stop him.

That was why she had to stop him getting too close.

Joanna took another step back, her feet slipping off the road and onto the grassy verge. "I warn you—"

"I was just going to give you my coat," the man said quietly. He was pulling it off, holding it in one hand. "You're cold, aren't you?"

Indecision flooded through Joanna's heart. She was cold. The icy night was starting to seep into her bones, and she knew it would be far harder to warm up once she lost the energy of her passionate fear.

Yet the idea of accepting anything from this man . . . giving him the idea she owed him . . .

"Here, take it," said the man flatly, throwing her the coat.

Joanna's instincts took over and she caught it. "But—"

"Put it on," the man said with a wry smile. "Then we can

talk."

It was on the tip of her tongue to say there would be absolutely no talking whatsoever. But like many things on the tip of Joanna's tongue, she did not permit the words to fall. She was not the sort of lady to speak her mind. Why would that change now, in the middle of a dark, French night?

The coat was warming. Joanna was not one to admit her private thoughts in any scenario, but as she pulled the heavy woolen garment around her, the cold sensation immediately started to melt away.

It smelt of him. Of a man. A powerful, arrogant man.

Joanna had been raised a lady, so she forced herself to meet his gaze. "Th-Thank you."

The man grinned. "It was hard, thanking me. Wasn't it?"

Joanna swallowed. *Yes*, she wanted to say. *You were the one who threatened me with a knife! You are the one who dragged me out here on a horse! You are the one standing there looking at me like . . . like . . .*

Instead, she said, "The servant. He said you were not the Duke of Fitzpaine."

The Duke of Fitzpaine laughed. "Oh, there'll always be Frenchies looking to stir trouble. I could sense immediately that it wasn't worth risking my life to convince a few French peasants who had managed to rise to the rank of officer that they were dining with an English gentleman of the blue blood."

Joanna nodded.

Well, that made sense. You could see just from the way the man held himself he was nobly born. There was an arrogance there far greater than that of the normal man.

Though of course, most gentlemen were unbearably arrogant to begin with.

"And you are?"

Joanna firmly ignored the question. It was not as though she owed him anything, did she? The man may be a duke, but he had hurt her. Grabbed her wrist, pulled her along, threatened her with a knife—

"You must have a name."

Joanna swallowed. It was not in her nature to be disobedient. Even when she had hated the orders her father had given her—dance with that gentleman, attend this card party, smile, smile, smile—she had obeyed.

The thought of disobeying was so unnatural, she was rather astonished it was within her grasp now.

"Why should I give you my name?" Joanna said softly.

Her body rebelled at her rudeness instantly. A strange rush of nausea stirred in her stomach, and she wished to goodness she were not such a wallflower.

Wallflowers were meant to stand at the sidelines at Almack's, she thought wretchedly. Not become kidnapped in goodness-knows-where, France!

The Duke of Fitzpaine's eyes raised. "I see. You don't wish to become acquainted with a duke?"

Joanna looked at her hands.

It was difficult to even countenance being rude to anyone, let alone a duke. She had been raised by her father to be polite, answer any question, and marry extremely well. But the thought of giving her name to this duke who evidently had no compunction in hurting her gave her just enough steel.

"What are you doing here?" Joanna said to her hands. "In France, I mean. With those officers."

She managed to look up, just for a moment, and saw a strange look flicker across the man's face. Something she could not put her finger on. An unwillingness to talk.

Ah. So she wasn't the only one hiding something.

The wind blew hard, rustling the leafless branches and making Joanna shiver again. This was ridiculous! How was it possible she was having a conversation on the side of a French road in the dark?

They needed to find shelter. *At least*, Joanna thought hastily, *she needed to find shelter.* Perhaps a kindly woman in a farmhouse would take her in. Somewhere far away from—

"My business is my own," the duke said firmly. "And I have given my name. Arthur Hebblethwaite, Duke of Fitzpaine. It would only be polite for you to give me yours."

Joanna silently fought against the truth of his words. Though she was loathe to admit it, he was right. She had been raised for Society, had come out, entered the *ton*, attended more than her fair share of parties. Even if she had hated every single minute of it, she knew what was expected of her.

Joanna bobbed a slight but still distinguishable curtsey. "Joanna . . . Epwin."

Well, he would not mind her borrowing his name, would he?

And it would be dangerous to give her real name. It was famous throughout London, after all, and there was surely a reward for her safe return. Not that she wanted this man, this duke, to think her a particularly convenient catch. Her dowry was not a bribe to make irritating men wish to wed her.

"And what are you doing here, Joanna Epwin?"

She could not help it. Against her better nature, against her character, Joanna lifted her gaze and glared at the arrogant man. "You brought me here." Heat flushed her cheeks the moment she spoke, but it was too late now. Joanna had surely offended him.

But the Duke of Fitzpaine laughed. "I suppose I deserved that. Come on, tell me the full story. How did an Englishwoman like you—any Englishwoman—end up with those louts?"

Shame flickered across Joanna's heart.

". . . an Englishwoman like you . . ."

Yes, she was well aware of her deficiencies. She was shy, nervous. She hated conversation, hated the false niceness Society demanded. She had no wish to pretend interest in other people and was just as quick to forget someone's name as remember it.

An Englishwoman like her—plain, with a shock of blonde hair that rarely behaved.

An Englishwoman like her.

"I'm waiting."

Joanna swallowed. How did he do it, this man? Was it just part and parcel of being a duke? Did all dukes have this domineering way of speaking, demonstrating to the world they were accustomed to getting everything they wanted, and at once?

"I was captured."

"That much is evident," said the unrelenting Duke of Fitzpaine. "Where were you captured from? Where is your family?"

And in that moment, an idea flashed through Joanna's mind. "I was captured in Paris while I was . . . was on my honeymoon."

Why she had lied, she did not know. Joanna had never lied before. At least, not a lie like this. Little white lies were practically a requirement of polite Society.

"Oh, I do adore your hat."

"What a charming son you have."

"Yes, I am having a marvelous time."

But a lie, a true lie? It had never crossed her mind, until she was faced with the handsome, irritating, dangerous duke before her and there was no one to stand between them.

No brothers, her father hundreds of miles away. Would the specter of a husband keep the Duke of Fitzpaine at bay?

"Honeymoon?" The man's voice was curious. Joanna glanced up to see his raised eyebrow. "You're not wearing a wedding ring."

She swiftly clasped her hands together, hiding the fourth finger on her left hand. "It was stolen."

"Stolen?"

"I have been captured by the French army and held as their prisoner," Joanna said, as haughtily as she could manage without her voice quavering. "You think it has been pleasant?"

"I see," he said slowly. "And where is your husband now?"

For the first time since she met this dangerous duke, Joanna almost smiled. "You know, I have no idea."

It was foolish. Madness!

Lying was not something young ladies were supposed to do. Joanna Bettencourt—Epwin, she must remember that—may be four and twenty, far past marriageable age in her father's consideration and frighteningly close to going on the shelf, but she was old enough to know not to lie.

And more than old enough to know what dangers could be found in the company of a duke. *That*, Joanna told herself, heart fluttering, *was why she had done it.*

Now the Duke of Fitzpaine believed her to be married, surely he would not touch her, would he? Would he aid her, perhaps, in returning to England? He should certainly treat her with the respect and cordiality a married woman—

"What a fortunate man your husband is," the duke said with a lazy smile. "God, yes."

Joanna flushed, almost walking backward through a hedgerow. "Stay away from me!"

"Mrs. Epwin, I didn't—"

"Don't touch me!" Joanna said, panic flooding her senses so utterly she was half convinced the man was before her, his hands already upon her. "I warn you—"

"Look, woman, I'm five feet away," came the voice of the astonished duke. "What on earth are you shouting for?"

Joanna managed to slow her breathing, blinking rapidly as the sight of the man—indeed, several feet from her—came into view.

Slowly, slowly, the tightness in her lungs lessened and Joanna could feel her fingers again. Oh, this was awful. What a terrible mess she had found herself in! And none of it was her fault, yet she would suffer through it all. What was she going to do now?

"Well," Joanna said shortly. "This is a fine mess you've got us in."

"I've got us in?" For some reason, the duke's voice was full of astonishment.

"Yes, you!" How could the man think she had anything to do with this disaster? "It was not I who stormed from the table! I did not grab at you and threaten you with a knife!"

Joanna raised her hands in horror and covered her mouth. *What did she think she was doing?* She had never shouted before.

She was a softspoken woman, always quiet. Even as a child there had been few tantrums, her shame and embarrassment at making a fuss preventing it. And now the first time ever she had raised her voice and truly shouted was at a duke?

Joanna tried to hold back the panic rushing through her, but it was impossible. Her head hurt, her heart was frantically beating, and she knew the man would be offended. How could he not? She had been so abominably rude!

No, the only recourse was to apologize. Apologize, and hope—

Joanna blinked. The Duke of Fitzpaine was laughing.

"Well, you're right enough there, I suppose," he said with a shrug. "Goodness, if I had known you were an Englishwoman—well, I may have rescued you anyway."

Joana swallowed. She was not contrary enough to say she did not need to be rescued. She had been in need of rescue, great need. If she had been helped by anyone else, in any other manner, she would certainly have been grateful.

But this charming, irritating, arrogant man?

No, she would certainly not lower herself to thank him. Even if he was a duke.

"Wh-What are you going to do now?" Joanna asked, dread tinging her tones.

She had just managed to meet his eye again but as she saw the unbridled desire, she looked away rapidly. She was all alone here. No one to protect her, no one to stop him—

"How did you end up with such brutes, anyway?"

Joanna swallowed. "I—they took me. In Paris."

"Took you?"

She closed her eyes, just for a moment, as the memories rushed in. The sudden noise in the hotel downstairs, the shouted French, the screams, the laughter as the soldiers pulled her away.

"What will you do now?" Joanna said aloud, opening her eyes. She would not permit herself to dwell on that time. Never again.

"Well, I think I'll make for England," the duke said breezily. "There's little here for me in France now, and it would be pleasant to speak God's own English all the time, not this dratted French."

Joanna blinked. *Had she heard that correctly? He wished to return to England?*

And hope, hope that she had quelled and forbidden herself to feel the moment she had been taken in Paris, rushed through her.

England. Home.

"Wonderful," Joanna said, her shoulders sagging with relief. "I have missed England greatly. I will be glad, I own, to see it again."

Even in the gloom she could see the Duke of Fitzpaine blinking with confusion.

"No—no, I meant me," said the man with a frown. "I'm going back to England. What you do is your own affair."

Joanna's mouth fell open. *The man could not be serious!*

Yet it appeared very much that he was. The duke turned on his heels and walked to the horse which had been waiting patiently in the middle of the road. He was organizing the reins, readying himself to mount.

He was going to leave her here!

And though Joanna hated drawing attention to herself, though she had no wish to take a step closer to the arrogant man who had caused her so much trouble, she knew it was a darn sight better than being abandoned.

Joanna forced herself to move. Each step was agonizing but eventually she reached the duke and grabbed his wrist—*much*, she thought wryly, *as he had grabbed hers less than an hour ago.*

"You cannot truly," she said, her breath short, "be thinking of leaving me here?"

CHAPTER THREE

5 February, 1811

I T WAS ALL Arthur could do not to scowl. "Isn't it my turn?"

He regretted the words the moment they had left his mouth. It wasn't particularly noble of him, was it?

Forget noble. It wasn't particularly manly. Arthur had never been one to complain, not out loud, but there was something about this woman that prickled at his good sense and made it disappear within a heartbeat.

Mrs. Epwin glanced down from the horse. There was an imperious look about her that Arthur both did not like and craved to see again.

"I thought dukes," she said primly, "were meant to be gallant."

Arthur nearly swallowed his tongue as he fought his better instincts. Or at least, his better instincts fought with his first instinct, which was to pull the woman from the horse and tell her being gallant did not mean walking half the length of France!

But he managed to stay silent. Mrs. Epwin's smile warmed.

Honestly! When she had almost stamped her foot last night and demanded he escort her to England, Arthur had been in half a mind to mount the horse and ride off without her.

He didn't need prim little wives without their husbands to take care of them slowing him down.

But he hadn't. Of course he hadn't. Arthur may not be an actual duke but he wasn't a cad. He wasn't about to leave Mrs. Joanna Epwin to her own devices in the middle of nowhere.

Even if she was hogging the time on the horse.

"I thought we were going to take turns," Arthur found himself saying.

He didn't know why he bothered. Though there was an inherent shyness in his female companion, every now and again a spurt of anger rose in her that could not be contained. He could see it, watching it spark across her face as though watching a firework.

And then it went. All that remained was a certain restraint Arthur did not understand.

Mrs. Epwin gave him a haughty expression. "I do not recall agreeing to such a proposition."

Arthur stamped along beside the horse in silence, temper brewing.

The trouble was, he couldn't disagree with her. When she had looked so pathetic last night in the dark, almost swallowed by his coat, Arthur knew he'd had no choice. Though she would slow him down and undoubtedly prove far greater a distraction than he could manage, Arthur had known he could never live with himself if he just left her here.

There were some things you did not need to be a duke to know were wrong.

So he had agreed. He would chaperone her to the nearest port, and that would be that. Arthur had a little coin, probably enough to get him passage to England. Clever Mrs. Epwin had not enquired about that, and he was not about to volunteer the knowledge.

The fact she had no coin on her was evident. Arthur had spent long enough looking at her and her gown to see she had no reticule—*to study her*, he told himself firmly. He had not been looking for any other reason.

There was nowhere upon her person that Mrs. Epwin could be hiding coin. She was going to get a sharp shock when they arrived at whatever port they were making for. When she realized he had absolutely no intention of helping her to England.

Arthur's conscience, battered and beleaguered, tried to put up a fight.

Was he truly going to leave her here in France? All alone?

But the man Arthur had been forced to become pushed aside all concerns.

He was the Duke of Fitzpaine. At least, that was who Mrs. Epwin thought he was. And he wasn't about to allow himself to get dragged into looking after a woman who hadn't even thanked him for rescuing her.

A prickle of discomfort seared his heart. *Well. At knifepoint. But still.*

"Besides, I would have thought you'd enjoy the exercise."

Arthur glanced up, despite himself, at the woman who looked far too comfortable sitting astride the horse. "What on earth do you mean, woman?"

Though her cheeks pinked, Mrs. Epwin apparently decided to ignore his rudeness. "I thought dukes loved exercise. Hunting, riding, that sort of thing."

"Yes, riding," said Arthur through gritted teeth. "I could not agree with you—"

"And I am sure you have had few opportunities to stretch your legs, as you wined and dined with French officers," Mrs. Epwin said quietly, not looking at him. "I would say you are in need of the exercise."

Arthur's jaw tightened, but he did not respond.

The cheek of the woman! Every time he was convinced she was a wallflower, she said something like that!

Something carefully curated to wound. He was no spy, nor a traitor. He wasn't in France merely to dine with French officers, he had been trying to find—

But he couldn't explain that. She wouldn't understand the need to find the Duke of Wincham. His desperation to find employment, and his foolish decision to pretend to be a Duke as he traveled. He wasn't even sure the Duke of Wincham would remember him. Who would remember a footman who only served him a few months?

And he wasn't, as she seemed to be implying, in need of losing any weight! The very idea!

Arthur gritted his teeth as he continued to walk alongside the woman on the horse. It would do no good arguing with her. He didn't need to know the woman more than four and twenty hours to be sure. All women were the same.

"How far is it? The coast, I mean," came Mrs. Epwin's quiet voice.

Arthur glanced up, despite himself, and his stomach lurched. *How was such a beautiful woman so . . . so reticent? So shy?*

It beggared belief. Now he was seeing her in the brightness of day, he could understand why the pretty little Englishwoman had been taken by the French in Paris, as she had described it. She was stunningly beautiful with a charm she did not seem to realize she possessed.

And that blonde hair! Golden, almost, it shone in the weak wintery sunlight so brilliantly sometimes Arthur could hardly bear to look at it.

Mrs. Epwin flushed at his gaze.

Arthur unclenched his jaw. She had asked about the distance to the coast. He had to focus on that. "I am not sure."

"What do you mean, you are not sure?"

What on earth did she think she meant? "Quite what I say. There is a distance between us and the coast, and I have not measured it."

It was tiredness, Arthur told himself, making him so rude. That was the only reason. Not that she was tantalizingly close as he walked alongside her. Not that he could still remember the sensation of her in his arms. Not the teasingly close movements of her shoulders right below his lips as her breath quickened—

"I would have thought you would know," came Mrs. Epwin's quiet voice. "You are a duke, after all."

Though irritation shot through him—*how was a duke supposed to know France like the back of his hand?*—Arthur quickly realized this was a blessing in disguise.

It was proof positive, as if he needed it, that the woman completely believed his story. He had half expected her to challenge him on what she had heard. *"I tell you, that is not the Duke of Fitzpaine! That's—Arthur? Arthur Hebblethwaite, is that you?"* After all, Laurent had yelled. The whole room had heard. It would have been impossible for her to ignore it.

She would have been well within her rights to accuse him of lying, to attempt to make him prove that he was the Duke of Fitzpaine.

But Arthur had remained unchallenged. It appeared Mrs. Epwin entirely believed him.

Joy rose within him. It was so easy. It was a wonder others didn't do this, too. There was so much gained by pretending to be a duke. All the benefits, yet none of the responsibility.

He should have done this years ago.

"Dukes have far more important things to be worrying about than geography," Arthur said imperiously, being sure to lift his nose in the air as he had seen his old master, the Duke of Wincham, do. "I have people for that."

People for that. *Sometimes the things he said didn't even make sense,* Arthur thought, stifling a laugh. It didn't matter. No one seemed to notice.

Perhaps dukes and earls and the lot of them just spoke in ridiculous riddles. Perhaps none of them truly knew what the others were saying, but they all kept quiet for fear of being found out.

"I see," said Mrs. Epwin softly.

Arthur saw her embarrassment, her awkwardness.

She was a shy one. There was no feigning that level of discomfort.

Perhaps if she knew he were not a duke . . . she would certainly be more comfortable. *Less concerned he was going to hurt her,* Arthur thought darkly. For that was what she had been afraid of last night, wasn't it?

"Stay back! I warn you—"

"I was just going to give you my coat. You're cold, aren't you?"

The thought of actually hurting a woman revolted him, dread tying itself in knots in his stomach. Arthur would never have actually hurt Joanna—Mrs. Epwin. Using her as a hostage of sorts had been nothing but bluster.

But she did not know that. Perhaps it was better that way.

Though Arthur did not relish the idea of lying to a lady, his false title would keep him safe. She would not think to disagree with him on the important things, and by the time they reached the coast, it would no longer matter.

He would leave her behind and travel back to England and the dearth of opportunity it offered him.

"You're not very gallant, are you?"

Arthur snorted at the shy words of his companion. "I was never the gallant sort."

That was true enough. Being born into poverty and having to fight for every crumb did not tend to lead a man into gallant actions. Arthur knew that, knew there was no shame in it. It had not been his fault his parents had been so poor.

"No, I thought not," said Mrs. Epwin faintly. She was looking directly ahead as she spoke, as though she were talking to herself, rather than the Duke of Fitzpaine. "You took me hostage."

Guilt seared through Arthur. Before he knew what he was doing, he found himself . . . *confessing.* "I would not have hurt you."

"Of course you wouldn't," Mrs. Epwin said lightly.

Her complete lack of belief in him stung, something Arthur had not expected. He was a duke! At least, he was pretending to be a duke. And dukes were not supposed to be injured by the disdain of young ladies.

Even if they were beautiful and alluring.

But for some reason, the fact that Mrs. Epwin thought so little of him irked Arthur to his very soul.

"I give you my word," he said quietly. "It was a ruse only. If they had rushed me, I would have thrust you toward them and attempted to make my escape."

For a moment, just a moment, she glanced over. "So you say."

Arthur swallowed his retort that she should trust a duke's word. "So I say."

They continued on in uncompanionable silence for some time. Arthur attempted to distract himself by looking at the French countryside. It was much like everywhere else. Barren fields, empty in the depths of winter. Hedgerows chattering with hungry birds. Leafless trees.

Yet it was still beautiful. That was something he had never lost from his time growing up in the wild countryside of England. Even in the darkness, when all seemed lost, when it seemed impossible to believe that spring would come again, there was beauty here. In the emptiness.

Arthur's roving gaze fell once again on the woman proving to be so troublesome. He should have left her at the table, he should never have grabbed her. Though really, he had saved her. Rescued her from capture. She still hadn't thanked him for that.

"Tell me about yourself."

Mrs. Epwin did not look at him. "No."

Arthur almost stumbled. "What do you mean, no?"

"Precisely what I say," came the woman's quiet reply.

"I just wish to know a little more about you and your husband," Arthur said cheerfully. Yes, that was it. Just pretend they were conversing at a dinner party. It was perfectly polite to enquire about a person, was it not?

Maybe it wasn't. Not actually being the Duke of Fitzpaine, he wasn't sure.

Mrs. Epwin still refused to look up. "I don't have to tell you anything."

Arthur shrugged, belying his growing irritation. "Oh, you don't have to do anything. That's the beauty of being an Englishman—or I suppose, an Englishwoman. We are free to do whatever we like. I just thought, as we could be spending a few days together—"

"A few days?" That got her attention. Mrs. Epwin met his gaze and something hot flared across Arthur's stomach. "You truly think it could be that long?"

How on earth was he supposed to know? "Perhaps. I thought we may both enjoy the time more if we . . . got to know each other."

It had not been his intention to make his words sound so seedy, but Arthur could not help it. She drew him to her, this woman. She wasn't doing it on purpose, at least from what he could see. But she was certainly alluring. She made him want to know her. To be close to her.

To touch her.

Just as he was about to reach out a hand to touch hers, Mrs. Epwin jerked the reins and the horse took a step away.

"I have no wish to *know* you, Your Grace," she said quietly, gaze averted.

Arthur sighed heavily, throwing his arms about him. "Well, it's not as though we have much else to entertain!"

"I don't need to be entertained," said Mrs. Epwin. "I just want to return to England."

"To your husband?"

"T-To my husband, yes," she said with a genteel nod.

Why was she so secretive about this man? "And his name is . . . ?"

For a moment there was naught but silence. Then, cheeks pink and gaze resolutely in the opposite direction, she said, "Mr. Epwin."

Oh, she was enough to drive any man to distraction! Not merely because she was so alluring, but because her very contrariness was coupled with a sweetness that made it very hard to argue against. How had this woman grown to be so shy, so retiring, yet speak with such sharpness?

"I don't understand you," Arthur said suddenly.

What had prompted him to be so open, he did not know. But the horse's clopping hooves continued with the same monotony as they had for hours, his stomach rumbled with hunger, and he was pushed to be far more direct than Mrs. Epwin would appreciate.

"You don't strike me as someone who is prim and proper," he continued, stuffing his hand in his breech pockets. "Yet you won't talk to me. I am a duke! Every woman in England wants to talk to a duke!"

"I am not in England."

Arthur almost laughed at the curt reply. *Well, he couldn't argue with that.*

As the three of them—himself, Mrs. Epwin, and the horse—meandered down the road that twisted to the left, he tried to examine her not from the perspective of one who had never been in Society, but from the view of a gentleman. He may not be a gentleman, but Arthur didn't intend for Joanna Epwin to ever discover that. And if he tried to look at her as a gentleman . . .

Well, hang it. She looked just the same. Just as awkward, just as shy. Just as unwilling to talk to him, just as happy to—

No, there was something there. Despite the hardships she had endured, Arthur had not heard her complain. She had railed against the way he had treated her, to be sure, but she was silent on the treatment of her captives. She was evidently a woman of great refinement. A woman who did not wish to make a nuisance of herself. A woman who wished to go through the world unnoticed and—

"Will you stop that?"

Arthur almost stumbled. Mrs. Epwin's words were soft, half spoken, half breathed. But they were clear enough.

"Stop what?" he replied with a frown.

"That," she said softly. "Looking at me."

Now that was interesting. Arthur had not noticed her observing him. She must have felt the intensity of his gaze on the back of her neck, somehow conscious he was examining her closely.

Interesting.

"Why?" Arthur said with a challenging laugh. "There's no husband here to stop me."

He regretted his words in an instant.

Mrs. Epwin flinched as though he had raised a hand to her, as though he had mortally wounded her. "Do not speak of my husband in that way."

Arthur swallowed. *He was not a brigand.* Not really. He did what he needed to get by, and if he could do it in comfort, well, why not? He had never before been spoken to like that by a woman. Something that tasted almost like guilt moved in his mouth.

"Your husband has nothing to fear from me," Arthur said softly.

And for the first time in a long time, Joanna Epwin met his gaze with fierce yet fearful eyes. "But do I?"

CHAPTER FOUR

JOANNA ALMOST SLUMPED over the horse's neck. "Oh dear."

There was nothing else to be said. She'd had such hopes all through this long day. For it had been merely four and twenty hours since she had been manhandled by a duke, rushed out of a room by knifepoint, forced onto a horse, forced to defend herself, and then had to demand not to be abandoned.

And now, from this outcrop, she could see all her hopes had been in vain.

"Oh dear," said the Duke of Fitzpaine, standing beside the horse.

It was clear what they were both looking at. The slight hill they had walked up had given them a view of the horizon and just how far the coast was. The shore was not around the next corner, as Joanna had been telling herself for the past two hours as the darkness started to drift in as the sun started to set. It wasn't even a mile away.

It was miles away. Hours and hours of riding. They would not reach the port tonight.

Joanna swallowed her frustration. She was accustomed to doing it. She rarely spoke her own mind, and any irritations had to be forced inside her, never to see the light of day.

It was just what she did.

Even so, it was particularly difficult to quell the panic and frustration. She had really thought, even if only for a few hours, she would end the day on a ship back to England.

Back to her home. Where she was valued.

Joanna almost smiled. *Valued a little too highly. Valued in the wrong way.*

"I did not expect it to be that distant," said the Duke of Fitzpaine with a heavy sigh. "Boll—bother, I mean."

Her cheeks tinged with heat at the incomplete curse. In truth, Joanna rather wished to swear herself.

The last few months had been a complete disaster, and hope had sparked when she believed she would be escorted back to London by a duke. That, at least, would be a fitting way to return.

"Well, we won't make it. Not tonight, at any rate."

Joanna gripped the reins. "I can see that."

"There's nothing else for it," said the duke, turning and starting back along the road the way they'd come.

Joanna blinked, then twisted around on the horse to watch him. Where on earth was he going? He could not seriously be thinking of returning to that manor where all the officers were, could he? *No, that was ridiculous. But the man had to have a plan, didn't he? He could be that idiotic—*

As though he had heard her thoughts, the duke called over his shoulder, "Come on! We passed an inn about ten minutes ago. We'll have to hope they have room."

For a moment, Joanna hesitated. She did not particularly appreciate being ordered about, though she supposed, as a duke, His Grace was accustomed to doing it.

He was obviously accustomed to being obeyed. When she did not turn the horse and begin to follow him, the Duke of Fitzpaine halted and looked back. "Aren't you coming?"

Joanna glanced at the shore. It was tantalizingly close, in a way. Almost as though she could reach out her hand and touch it. Dropping the rein with her right hand she reached out, heart aching. *So close, yet so far.*

"We'll never make it. Not tonight."

She returned her hand to the reins. "I know that."

"Then what are you waiting for?" the Duke of Fitzpaine asked cheerfully. "I could certainly do with a meal, even if you're not interested in a bed."

Joanna's stomach rumbled in response. It had been almost a full day since she had eaten, and she could not pretend she was not hungry. Even if she would have to suffer through the indignity of being asked even more questions by the nosy duke.

"To your husband?"

"T-To my husband, yes."

"And his name is . . . ?"

Why she had not responded to his innocent questions, she did not know. Joanna had never been a particularly bold woman. The very thought had mortified her. But somehow, with this duke, she found herself rebelling against anything he wanted. Even if what he wanted made sense.

"We can be in the warm within fifteen minutes, eating within twenty," he called to her. "Come on, Mrs. Epwin!"

Joanna flushed at the false name but there was nothing she could do. The man may be grating, but he was right. And she was hungry.

"I wish we could have made it to the coast," she found herself saying softly as she turned the horse around and followed the duke.

He nodded. "I know, but continuing on in this darkness would be madness."

"We walked through the last night," Joanna pointed out, half astonished at her boldness.

The Duke of Fitzpaine chuckled. "Yes, and much good that did us! Half the time we were going in the wrong direction and my bones ache. You can't tell me you wouldn't say yes to a good bedding."

Heat poured through Joanna's veins. *The very idea!* "I-I—I d-do not know wh—"

"Oh, hell, I didn't mean it like that," the duke said hastily, though that did not explain why there was such a grin on the man's face. "You know I didn't—"

"I have absolutely no idea what you could possibly be referring to," Joanna managed, with great effort, without a quaver in her voice.

"Of course you didn't."

Joanna firmly ignored the teasing air in the man's tone.

He may be a duke, and he may get away with speaking however he liked to his friends and his—his women, back in England! But she was not going to let him speak to her like that!

Thankfully, Joanna's eyes swiftly alighted on flickering lights in the distance. Lights coming from a large building, right on the side of the road.

"The inn," she breathed with relief.

Though she would fain not admit it to the irritating man, she was exhausted. Tiredness leaked from her very bones, and she knew if she did not rest soon, she could no longer ride.

Guilt rushed through her. And she had not been the one walking.

"Ah, the inn," the Duke of Fitzpaine said heartily. "Excellent."

It was indeed excellent. Joanna almost fell from the horse with fatigue, nearly collapsing into the waiting arms of—

"I do not need your help," Joanna said, stumbling back, just managing not to fall.

The Duke of Fitzpaine allowed his hands, which had risen to catch her, to fall to his side. "Of course."

Somehow it was even more infuriating when he simply agreed with her. Joanna didn't know what it was about him that drew out this side of her—it was something she had never been before. But whenever the Duke of Fitzpaine opened his mouth, she felt the need to argue with him. It was most mysterious.

"I'll see to the horse, you go inside into the warm," came his next words.

This, at last, was something Joanna could agree with.

The inn was busy, the hallway where she now stood crowded, and the clientele appearing genteel. Not that she would have quibbled if it were a more lowly establishment. At this moment, Joanna would take any opportunity to eat and sleep.

"Right."

Joanna started at the sudden noise.

"Nervous, aren't you?" grinned the Duke of Fitzpaine who had appeared behind her.

Joanna swallowed. She was, and she only seemed to be getting more nervous the longer she was in his company. But she wasn't about to reveal that innermost thought.

"You startled me," she said in a whisper.

The man shrugged, grin remaining. "Whoops. Shall we find a table?"

Though he was most exasperating, Joanna had to own—in the solitude of her own mind—it was much easier navigating the world with a duke by one's side.

She would have remained in the hallway for an age, waiting for someone to notice her. If the innkeeper had offered her a leaf on a plate, she would have eagerly accepted it. If no rooms had been available, she would have meekly requested shelter in the stable. And if that had been refused, she would not have argued.

The Duke of Fitzpaine could not have been more different.

"I am the Duke of Fitzpaine," he thundered at the poor serving maid who approached them. "And I demand the very best food, the best wine available, and a room—"

"Two rooms," hissed Joanna, cheeks scalding.

"Ah, yes, I quite forgot," said the duke with a wink as they sat at a table by a window.

Joanna looked at her hands in her lap, scalded with shame. How did he think it acceptable to look at her like that—to say things like that?

"—two rooms, then, and I want the food as soon as possible. Go on with you!"

Without looking up, she was conscious of the serving maid disappearing off in a flurry of panicked skirts.

Yes, he did have that effect on people, Joanna could not help but think. He had been having that effect on her ever since she had first been seated beside him. But she was a lady. She did not have to permit that sort of behavior. She was immune to it. She—

"You look remarkably beautiful in candlelight."

Heat flushed into her cheeks. "Keep your insults to yourself."

"My insults—. My dear Mrs. Epwin, it is not only your husband who can appreciate a beautiful woman," said the Duke of Fitzpaine with ease.

The ease of the lie she had told weighed heavily on Joanna's heart.

"I was captured in Paris while I was . . . was on my honeymoon."

It had been a slip of the tongue, a defensive reflex she had intended only to protect. Yet it was strange, to sit here with a duke, eating the plate of roast pheasant and vegetables the serving maid had brought, knowing their brief acquaintance was built on a lie.

Mrs. Epwin, indeed!

"The wine is really rather good," mused the Duke of Fitzpaine, glancing at the bottle. "You are sure you won't try any?"

Joanna shook her head. She was in more than enough trouble already without drinking French wine and losing all inhibitions around a man like him.

"So," he said, twisting his wine glass in his fingers. "Tell me about your family."

Joanna risked glancing up, just for a moment. Her whole body responded to the look the Duke of Fitzpaine was giving her.

Exhilaration flickered through her collarbone, soaring up her shoulders and tingling up her neck. Something shivered in her fingers as anticipation, though she knew not for what, quivered in her bones.

How on earth did he do that?

A teasing grin slipped onto the duke's lips and Joanna swiftly looked at her half-finished meal.

Just one more day, she thought, and she would be on a ship, avoiding him in her cabin. That was all she had to endure. That was how long she had to resist.

"I suppose your family will be missing you in England? Worried about you, I'd say."

Joanna hesitated. No one would be missing Mrs. Joanna Epwin. The woman was an invention.

Miss Joanna Bettencourt, heiress?

She was surprised a search party had not already found her.

Wondering just how much of the truth she should reveal to this man whose very presence seemed to act as a magnet for women—Joanna spotted five shooting the tall gentleman covert glances—she tried to collect herself.

The last thing she needed was a duke to know she was worth fifty thousand pounds.

She had met a few dukes, while in London. The Duke of Axwick had been ice itself, and the Duke of Penshaw had disappeared from polite circles for a while then surfaced with a bride who appeared rather uncouth. At least, that's what Joanna's father had said.

Almost all the other dukes she had met had one thing in common: they needed money.

Being a duke, it appeared, was an expensive business. Joanna did not understand it—did they not own land?—but knew she was coveted only for her dowry, and never herself.

Not that she'd ever revealed enough of herself to a gentleman for him to know her, Joanna thought wistfully.

She met the Duke of Fitzpaine's eyes and saw the force in his gaze. His determination, his absolute will, the certainty in him that he would get his own way. If he knew how much she was worth, would he not force her to marry him? Would she not be trapped, tied to him forever, this man who knew nothing about manners, gallantry, or kindness?

"I said," the Duke of Fitzpaine said, lifting his glass to his lips, "does your family not miss you?"

He sipped at the dark red liquid and Joanna tried to smile. A small amount of conversation, then. That could not hurt, could it?

"I do not imagine my family are that interested in my whereabouts," she lied.

Then shivered. *It was not a lie. Not entirely.*

How she wished it was. Her mother, had she lived, would probably have wished to discover her precious daughter. Her one child. But her father had seen her as naught but a method by which to connect to a noble family. The more noble, the better.

He would, Joanna thought wryly, *have been delighted at the idea of his daughter dining with a duke. Even in these circumstances.*

She had expected Fitzpaine to question her further, demand more details. What she did not expect was for him to nod sagely.

"Ah, yes," he said softly, swallowing a mouthful of pheasant. "I know all about that."

Joanna blinked. He could not be in earnest. The Duke of Fitzpaine? She had never heard of the dukedom, to be sure, but there were plenty of places in the far north of England she had never heard of, and there was something of a lilt in his accent. Something that was definitely not southern English.

"I myself have been disowned by my family," said the Duke of Fitzpaine nonchalantly, as though they were discussing the weather.

Joanna's mouth fell open. *Surely not!* She had never heard any gossip about a duke being disowned! Who could he be disowned by—his mother, a sibling?

She laughed, hardly knowing what to say. "Well, I cannot imagine that is much of an inconvenience."

Her breath was taken away by the intensity of his gaze. The duke had looked up and . . . well, it wasn't a glare. It wasn't that macabre, or that menacing. But it shot right to Joanna's heart. It was a look that told her he had known pain—true pain—and had never quite reconciled with it. It was a look that told her, somehow, he was alone in the world.

Her heart skipped a beat, her body rushed with heat, the inn started spinning—

And then the man looked away as though nothing had happened.

Joanna had to remind herself to take a breath. She had almost jested with a duke, and look where it had got her!

Out of touch with reality, she told herself firmly. Dreaming she'd shared a moment with a man far nobler than she would ever be.

"What do you mean?" the Duke of Fitzpaine asked the remainder of his pheasant.

Joanna had to take a couple of breaths to ensure her voice was strong enough to reply. "I merely meant . . . well, you are a duke. You must have friends, connections. Even without your immediate family, you are one of the most powerful men in the country."

And for some reason, the man flushed. "Of course. Yes, I— you are right."

For the first time since they had met, Joanna examined him closely.

Not just his looks. She was all too conscious the man was handsome. If she were not so afraid of him, perhaps she would be caught in his trap, but so far she had avoided it. No, Joanna looked deeper. At the way he was holding himself. The way he sat, the way his eyes darted about the place as though—as though he were afraid.

Perhaps she was not the only one keeping secrets.

"You're examining me."

Joanna started. "I am not—"

"There's no point in lying to me, Mrs. Epwin," said the duke with a laugh.

"I can assure you, Your Grace—"

"Fitzpaine."

The conversation was moving so rapidly, Joanna was struggling to keep up. What did he want from her now? To hear his name slip from her lips?

She was being ridiculous. This was not a dastardly deed, a mystery, or anything like that. This situation was a farce, perhaps, but it was a real one. Soon she would be on a ship and she would never have to think about him again.

"I don't . . . I think it better if I call you 'Your Grace,' don't you?" she said awkwardly.

There was a teasing note in his voice. "Not at all. In fact, I think I'd prefer it if you called me Arthur."

Joanna's stomach swooped. "Well, Fitzpaine, I suppose we will agree to disagree."

For an instant, he held her gaze with a glare. Then he roared with laughter.

His merriment was so infectious, she found herself laughing with him. What choice did she have? And she was tired, and the whole situation seemed ridiculous. Here she was, dining with a duke who thought her a married woman! Who had no idea she was an heiress!

"Are you finished?"

Joanna looked at her plate. She could hardly remember eating a single bite, but the meal had gone. She must have been far more hungry than she thought. "I suppose I am."

"In that case, I suggest we repair to our room."

Her stomach dropped to her knees. "Room?"

"Rooms, sorry," Fitzpaine said with a wink as he rose. "Can't blame a man for trying."

She could blame him for the scalding color of her cheeks. Joanna hoped, as they stepped through the dining area and up the stairs to the bedchambers, the color would not be too obvious. Her cheeks were so hot, she was certain that with her pale complexion she was glowing.

"Here I am," said Fitzpaine smartly, knocking on a door to his left. "And you are right beside me."

Joanna opened her door nervously. "And . . . and there is not a connecting door?"

She regretted asking the question immediately.

Fitzpaine grinned. "Wouldn't that be nice? Sorry to disappoint you, Mrs. Epwin, but I'm afraid you will be quite safe from me in there."

Joanna glanced into the room. It was serviceable, almost pleasant in her current state of exhaustion. A large bed tucked into one corner, a gas lamp which had been lit, and wide curtains covering what she had to assume was a window. And the bed looked more inviting with each passing moment.

"Good night, Mrs. Epwin."

Joanna jumped. "Wh—oh. Good night, Your . . . Fitzpaine."

Heart hammering at the intimacy he had corralled her into, she stepped inside the bedchamber and slammed the door behind her. There was a key in the lock. She turned it.

Joanna waited, hardly able to breathe, and listened. There was a chuckle on the other side of the door, then footsteps. A sound to her left of a door opening and closing. The squeak of someone clambering onto a bed. Silence.

Slowly, as though she had not been given permission to be in the bedchamber, Joanna stepped as lightly as she could over to her own bed. The mattress was most comfortable.

Tiredness finally overwhelming her, she allowed herself to fall onto the bed and looked at the ceiling.

Other ladies, Joanna told herself sternly, *would be attempting to catch a duke.* They would be taking every advantage of this situation and hoping to make the man—well, not necessarily fall in love.

Love, she was certain, was not something a duke knew much about.

But the point was, other ladies would see this as an opportunity. A chance to become a duchess.

How fortunate, Joanna thought with a flicker of guilt in her chest, *she was in no way attracted to the Duke of Fitzpaine.*

CHAPTER FIVE

6 February, 1811

"OH, THANK GOD," Arthur breathed. "We made it."

He had not intended to speak. The gusty winds were so strong, he was half sure Joanna—Mrs. Epwin, as he was supposed to call her—had not heard him. It had been fortunate indeed that he'd managed to barter a coat from some poor Frenchman who had been in greater need of the silver dagger than he was, for the wind would surely have chilled him to the bone.

Whether she had heard him or not, however, he could see her expression was very much how he felt.

"The shore," Mrs. Epwin said from atop the horse.

Arthur had been certain the path would gradually wend its way to the ocean, even if after a few turns he had wondered whether he was correct. There had been no other road in that direction, however, and after two hours of following it—ignoring Mrs. Epwin's sniffs—they had made it.

The small seaside town roared with life after the quiet of the countryside. Fisherman chattered away in loud French, mending their nets while their wives or daughters hauled the fish into town, ready for what appeared to be market day. There were shouts across the boats bobbing in the small natural harbor, seagulls squawking above them, children rushing about, hawkers attempting to sell pies and ale and, as far as Arthur could tell, women.

A lazy grin crept over his face. *The world really wasn't that different, was it?*

Other than the language, he could have been standing in any seaside town in Kent.

"Good," Mrs. Epwin said primly. "About time."

Arthur shot her a glare but managed to rearrange his face into a sycophantic and polite smile by the time she looked at him.

Well, hell's bells, he had been doing his best! It wasn't his fault the coast had been so much farther than he had thought. They had walked—he had walked, that was, as she had ridden—for hours. It was not as though she had suffered.

It was going to be a relief to rid himself of this Mrs. Epwin. Oh, she was pretty. Perhaps if she were a little less shy and a little more exuberant, he could enjoy her conversation. He certainly enjoyed looking at her.

But the way she expected everything to be just so, her horror at anything other than the most genteel option?

Now that, Arthur could live without.

Besides, pretending to be a duke in her presence was exhausting. It was all very well doing it before the French. They had no real idea how an English duke was supposed to be. Arthur could be himself, but with far more haughtiness. But Mrs. Epwin?

She gave off the impression of not only being a member of Society, but perhaps even one who had been presented at St James's Court. She was a woman who could, at any moment, realize the truth.

Or rather, the lie.

"What a relief to arrive," Mrs. Epwin said, almost to herself, as he walked and she rode down the main street of the coastal town.

Arthur snorted. "I did not believe my company was that

poor."

A spark of irritation shot through him. He was not one to think a great deal of himself. He knew his place, his true place, here on the ground. She'd made that perfectly clear.

The trouble was, Joanna—Mrs. Epwin—wasn't supposed to think that. She was supposed to think he was a high born, wealthy, noble man. Yet here she was, practically crowing over him that she was delighted to be rid of his company!

"I did not say poor—I would not be so uncouth as to remark directly upon it," Mrs. Epwin said, just a hint of sharpness in her tone.

"I apologize for rescuing you from the French and bringing you here," Arthur snapped.

That got her attention. "I-I didn't—I thought—I never said—"

"You did not need to say it, Mrs. Epwin," Arthur said with a brittle sort of cheerfulness he could see irritated the woman. "Your demeanor toward me the last two days has said it all."

They stepped out onto the port as he spoke, the weak wintery sunlight on the ocean dazzling him for a moment.

After blinking several times and regaining his bearings, he was astonished to find Mrs. Epwin close to him. Remarkably close. She had somehow dismounted from the horse in one smooth movement he had barely registered and was now standing but a foot from him.

"I do apologize, Your Grace," she said softly, raising nervous eyes. "I am . . . that is to say, being shy, I rarely . . . . Thank you."

Arthur's mouth went dry as he stared at the beautiful woman.

Well, hang it all! That was not what he had expected. It was much more difficult to be irritated with a woman who said all that.

She was shy. He kept forgetting that. Arthur had never been shy a moment in his life, and it was hard to imagine wandering through the world without the confidence he had been born with. Let alone the confidence he was borrowing as the false

Duke of Fitzpaine.

"Ah," Arthur said awkwardly.

What was he supposed to say to that? Was he supposed to take her hand, kiss it?

The thought warmed Arthur's heart. Now that was an intriguing idea. Any excuse to touch Mrs. Epwin again would be one he—

"What should we do with the horse?"

Arthur blinked. *Horse? What was she talking about?*

"Fitzpaine?" Mrs. Epwin was waving a hand before his eyes.

Arthur did not know why. He could see perfectly well. His gaze was dazzled by the brilliance of her smile, the gloss of her hair. It was his mouth that was having difficulty.

"Arrghhg," he mumbled.

Mrs. Epwin blinked. "I'll dispose of the horse."

It was only after she walked away, leading the mare which had taken them from the French camp all the way to the sea, that Arthur swallowed and regained his senses. It was nothing to do with the fact he was no longer stupefied by her mere presence, he tried to tell himself. He wasn't completely lost to the presence of a beautiful woman.

Still, it was a strange look that she gave him when Mrs. Epwin returned. There was something different about her, Arthur was certain, but he couldn't put his finger on it.

Though he'd quite happily put a finger on her.

"Fitzpaine, are you quite well?"

"Well?" Arthur said, then shook his head as though ridding water from his ears. "Yes, yes, I'm perfectly fine, thank you. No need to worry about—what in God's name did you do with that horse?"

His brain had finally caught up with him. The woman had walked off with a horse and returned without one. The woman hadn't pushed the horse into the sea, had she?

"I sold her," said Mrs. Epwin promptly.

Arthur's mouth fell open. "Sold her?"

"Of course. I doubt we wish to return to England with her," Mrs. Epwin said, as though explaining a very simple mathematics problem to a small child who was liable to have a tantrum at any moment. "I received fifty livres for her."

Arthur's eyes widened. "Fifty—"

Well, the woman certainly knew her way around French, he thought begrudgingly as Mrs. Epwin flushed in the intensity of his gaze. Clever, too. He had the funds for the passage on a ship to England, and though they had never discussed it, he was half certain Joanna—*he really had to remember to call her Mrs. Epwin*—had been penniless.

She wasn't penniless now.

"There are quite a few ships, aren't there?"

Arthur forced himself to pay attention. He was supposed to be the duke here. He may not have the lineage, but he could pretend—and he needed to get his act together!

"Let's find the harbor master," he said grandly, as though this was something he did all the time. "The man will be able to inform us of the fastest ship to England."

Mrs. Epwin nodded and lifted her hand in one elegant movement.

Just about an inch before she touched Arthur's arm, she flushed and stepped away.

Arthur's mouth was dry as his gaze snapped forward and he pretended he had not seen the instinctual movement of the woman who was evidently a part of the *ton*. Why, she had been about to take his arm! As though they were walking in Hyde Park, or about to . . . what was it these ladies called it? Take a turn about the room?

He could not conceive of a situation less like that! Here they were, both with funds but with little else to recommend them, trying to find a ship in a small French port to take them to England.

And there was the possibility they would not find one. Arthur's stomach twisted. They'd have to take a ship going as far up the French north coast as possible, then attempt to return to England from there. Not that he had much to return to. But after the debacle with those French captains, he doubted whether the Duke of Fitzpaine would be welcome in France any longer.

It was not difficult to find the harbor master. The man was wandering around with what appeared to be the largest gold chain on his pocket watch Arthur had ever seen—though that wasn't saying much.

"Ah, good afternoon, sir," Arthur said in perfect, though terribly accented French. "Are you the harbor master here?"

The man beamed. "Monsieur Garnier, at your service, monsieur and madame."

Arthur glanced at the woman beside him and saw her flush.

Well, it was technically true, wasn't it? Mrs. Epwin was married. She wasn't married to him, but that was neither here nor there. The man didn't need to know.

"Excellent, I am glad to hear it," Arthur said, turning back to Monsieur Garnier. "Tell me, Garnier—" he heard Mrs. Epwin's intake of breath. *Was that wrong? Couldn't a duke call a man by his surname?* "—we seek a ship to take us to England. Which—"

"Ah, you want the *Liberté*," Monsieur Garnier said knowledgably, nodding in the direction of a ship just behind them.

Arthur turned as one with Mrs. Epwin and grinned at the ship bobbing in the waves. It was large, perhaps the largest ship here. It appeared to be in good shape, though Arthur would have to admit he did not really know what he was looking at.

Still. There was one here, and it was going to England. That was all they needed.

"How long will it take, Monsieur Garnier?" Mrs. Epwin was asking.

Arthur almost rolled his eyes. Of course she was going to be as polite as possible. Was that something that ladies in the *ton* did? Or was that a peculiarity of Mrs. Epwin herself?

"Only a week, madame," said the harbor master, puffing out his chest proudly.

"A—a week? Truly, as long as that?" Mrs. Epwin said in genuine horror.

Arthur cleared his throat. "You have to remember, we are in the south of France," he said in English in a low voice as Monsieur Garnier blustered in French. "This isn't Paris. This isn't going to be a short crossing. We are much farther from England than I believe you thought."

A dark flush covered Mrs. Epwin's cheeks. Arthur did not know why. He had not intended to shame her, yet this woman was right on the verge of offense at any given moment.

Shy. That was what she called it.

Well, she certainly was that. But there was something more, Arthur was certain. There was a secret there. She was not telling him the entire truth.

"—Captain Toussaint will be happy to speak with you," Monsieur Garnier was saying. "In fact, you are fortunate. There is only—"

"Yes, yes, wonderful, thank you very much, Monsieur Garnier," Arthur said hurriedly, patting the man on the arm and nodding his thanks.

They didn't have time to hear the harbor master's thoughts on the ships to England, after all. They knew there was only one. All they needed to do now was find this Captain Toussaint, book passage, and settle into their respective cabins.

Arthur bowed then turned away from Monsieur Garnier, but not before—

"That was abominably rude!" hissed Mrs. Epwin beside him as they approached the *Liberté*.

"I needed some information, and he provided it. I had no further use for him."

As he spoke, exhilaration rushed through his veins. Yes, that was how the dukes of the world treated others, wasn't it? And why shouldn't he do the same? Why did it always have to be the nobles who could get away with rudeness?

It appeared, however, that in Mrs. Epwin's eyes at least, he had not got away with his rudeness.

"Well, I think it was shameful," she said, cheeks brick red as they reached the *Liberté*. "He was about to tell us something important and you—"

"He was going to repeat that this was the only ship going to England, and that is no interest nor use to me," Arthur said smoothly. *Goodness, she was a moral one, wasn't she?* "Ah, Captain Toussaint, I presume?"

Relief rushed through Arthur as the man nodded.

At last. After all this nonsense in France, it was best to return to England. He could travel to the very north and continue his duke pretense there. No Society ever ventured that far. He could find someone who believed his story, and—

"You are intolerable," Mrs. Epwin hissed.

Arthur grinned. "Probably. So, Captain Toussaint, you are for England?"

The captain nodded. "I am indeed."

"We are ready to book passage," said Arthur smartly, reaching into his waistcoat for the notes he had carefully secreted there a while ago. He had always known it would be useful to keep these stolen francs on him. After all, one never knew what was coming next.

"The Duke of Fitzpaine and I—"

"Goodness, truly, a duke? We are honored."

Arthur grinned as he straightened. He had not expected Joanna to ensure the entire crew knew they were transporting a duke so easily. He could not have done it better himself.

"You are in luck," Captain Toussaint said. "Very fortunate indeed."

And suddenly a strange sense of foreboding rushed across Arthur's skin, prickling every inch of it. A rush of something odd rocked his stomach, twisting it in a knot, and his heart skipped a beat.

This was wrong. Every instinct told him that this was not, as he had thought, the solution to their problems.

They should leave. Now.

"Joanna," Arthur breathed.

But Mrs. Epwin, despite the use of her first name, did not appear to heed the Duke of Fitzpaine's words. "Why do you call us fortunate, Captain?"

Arthur groaned. He did not need to hear the man speak. He already knew no good would come of it.

For months, he had traveled around France being greeted here, there, and everywhere as the Duke of Fitzpaine. People had invited him to stay, dined with him, paid off any small gambling debts he had accrued, then he moved on. Usually in the middle of the night.

It was accepting Captain Blanchet's invitation which had done it, Arthur thought bitterly. That was when this had all gone wrong.

That had been when he had first encountered Joanna Epwin.

"Why, because we only have the one cabin left," Captain Toussaint said cheerfully. "It is indeed fortunate that it is a married couple who wishes to take it!"

Arthur's heart sank.

What was it the harbor master had said—or tried to say?

"In fact, you are fortunate. There is only—"

He had presumed the man was repeating his information that there was only one ship traveling to England. Now Arthur knew better. Now he realized Monsieur Garnier was attempting to tell them something completely different.

There was only one cabin.

Try as he might, Arthur could not stop himself looking at Mrs. Epwin, whose flushed cheeks had never recovered from his rudeness to the harbor master. Her eyes flashed with something he had never seen before.

Not boldness—that was not quite right. But a certainty, a determination that what she was about to do was precisely the right thing. The only thing.

Another sense of foreboding swept over him. What on earth was she intending to do?

Perhaps she was about to persuade the captain to give her the only cabin.

The thought flashed through his mind before he could stop it. Well, it would not tally with his experience of Mrs. Epwin's character, but he supposed if she were truly desperate she might.

And a traitorous, most ungallant thought followed it. Could he, Arthur, not offer the captain more money to have the cabin to himself? There would be another ship going to England from this port any day now, Arthur reasoned wretchedly. And it would be pleasant not to continuously fight his attraction to her.

But leaving Joanna Epwin behind did not settle with his conscience. This came as a great surprise to Arthur, who had never considered himself burdened with such a thing before. Looking at her, her blonde hair shimmering in the sunlight, the rosebud mouth parting as though to speak, Arthur realized he would have to be a gentleman. Even if he wasn't actually a gentleman.

"I see," Arthur said heavily, hating that he was going to have to spend another few nights here in this blasted place. "Well, in that case—"

"Oh, is that not wonderful news?" Mrs. Epwin said brightly.

Arthur's mouth fell open. He would have spoken, too, if it had not been for the hand which had slipped into his own.

He looked down. Mrs. Epwin's hand. *What the devil did she think she was doing?*

"After losing my wedding ring, it is such a joy to see our luck is turning! My husband and I will happily take the cabin, Captain Toussaint," Mrs. Epwin said cheerfully. "You know what they say, where there's a will, there's a way. Oh, darling!"

And before Arthur could say a word, before he could digest what was happening, before his mind could even fathom the sensation of her warm fingers entwined in his—

All thoughts stopped.

Mrs. Epwin was kissing him.

And not just a peck on the cheek, either. That would surely have sufficed, thought Arthur wildly, yet she had done far more than that. Her lips were pressed against his own, her whole body leaning into him, and she was kissing him, kissing him passionately, kissing him as though they had been restraining themselves for years and this was finally their chance to be together.

Well, he wasn't a monk, was he?

Arthur's free hand curled around her immediately, pulling Joanna—for he could no longer think of her as Mrs. Epwin—into a tighter embrace. His hand clasped her waist, relishing the warmth of her, and he tilted his chin to take the kiss deeper.

By the time the kiss finally ended, Arthur was unsurprised to see Captain Toussaint's face was just as red as Joanna's.

Well, well. That would take some consideration.

"A pleasure to welcome a newly wedded couple to my ship," coughed the captain.

Arthur cleared his throat. He should say something, he knew, but it was impossible to think. Who could have guessed that the prim, proper, and shy Joanna Epwin had it in her?

"Well then," Joanna said rather breathlessly. "Shall we board, husband?"

Arthur coughed. "I—I suppose we should, after that display."

There was just a flicker of embarrassment in her gaze as she met his own, and she turned and started walking up the gangplank onto the ship.

Arthur stood, dazed. How was he supposed to walk after that? How was the world supposed to continue turning as though nothing had occurred?

The captain coughed. "Mighty fine woman you have. Duchess, I mean. Your Grace."

"I—I suppose I do," said Arthur, a grin turning up the corners of his mouth. "Dear God. Right."

CHAPTER SIX

JOANNA WAS SHAKING by the time she and the duke—*the duke! The Duke of Fitzpaine!*—were shown into the cabin.

"Our best cabin," Captain Toussaint was saying by the door, where Fitzpaine had thrust out an arm to prevent him entering. "See? The largest bed, perfect for the happily married couple! A desk there, and a dressing table for madame, and these two chairs, perfect for . . ."

Joanna could barely take it in. This was going to be their home for the next week.

A week. Seven days. And seven nights.

"Well then. Shall we board, husband?"

"I—I suppose we should, after that display."

Her muscles were taut across her shoulder blades, and a throbbing in her head refused to abate as Joanna sat carefully on the end of the bed.

The duke was still trying to make the captain leave. "Yes, we have all we need—"

"And if you think of anything else you need, please be sure to—"

"You will be the first to know, Toussaint. My—Joanna is tired, we must rest—"

"Any particular food you would like? There is still time for my cook to go to the market, anything you wish—"

Joanna closed her eyes as she twisted her hands in her lap, trying to block out the sound of the exhausted Fitzpaine and the obsequious captain.

What had she done?

Well, she had said words she would never have believed possible in her life. She had acted more boldly than Joanna had thought was in her. And just when she had seen the captain had been unconvinced of their affection, she had done the only thing she could think of.

She had kissed a duke. Passionately.

Joanna swallowed, eyes still shut as Fitzpaine continued to argue with the captain.

What had possessed her? It was the most scandalous thing she had ever done. She had never even thought of doing anything like that before. If her father—

But her father was not here, Joanna told herself firmly, eyes snapping open to stare at the wooden wall. And she had not done anything wrong.

Well. She had. She had kissed a man who was unmarried. If he had any idea that she too was unwed, there would be scandal the moment they returned to London. They would be forced to wed! A man, forced to marry her, forced to spend his days with her. And his nights.

Joanna knew she could not bear it. So few gentlemen enjoyed her company even at the card table. Was she truly to be condemned to spending a life with a man bored every minute in her presence?

"—thank you, Captain Toussaint," Fitzpaine was saying firmly, slowly closing the door before the rapidly speaking man.

"—any time of day or night—"

The door snapped shut.

"Thank God," the duke sighed. "I thought—"

"Hush!" Joanna said swiftly.

For once in his life, Fitzpaine did not disagree with her. Instead, he pressed an ear to the door. After a minute, he nodded.

"A clever thought," he said ruefully, turning to lean against the door. "The blackguard was waiting to listen. Well."

Joanna swallowed. Slowly, she allowed herself to fall back onto the bed.

Dear God. What had she done?

The ship's ceiling was a dark wood that appeared to have been oiled carefully. It was pleasant, just for a moment, to stare at it and pretend nothing had happened. Even if Joanna could still feel the pressure of Fitzpaine's lips on hers.

She swallowed. She had not wished to spend another day in France, another day as someone's captive. He could protest all he liked, but the duke had not rescued her from those French. She had simply been useful, and she was tired of being useful. She wanted to go home.

And she had seen the look in his eye. He had been about to take the cabin for himself and leave her there!

The Duke of Fitzpaine was not so clever as he thought.

"So," came his voice, tinged with mirth. "Do you mind explaining what happened?"

Joanna blinked, wishing a sense of calm could wash over her. But she seemed to be entirely made of panic and terror. Here she was, on a ship with countless men, none of whom would respect her if they discovered she was unmarried. Unmarried and unprotected.

And then there was the duke. Joanna forced herself not to look at him. She wasn't sure she would be able to even speak if faced with his handsome smirk. The man was intolerable, yet there had been no other choice. She would be his duchess for the journey and that was all. When they arrived at England, they would go their separate ways and she would never have to be subjected to his nonsense ever again.

Joanna started. What on earth did she think she was doing, lying on the bed before him? Lying on a bed? She was practically inviting him in!

Standing so swiftly her head spun, Joanna backed against the wall and tried to put as much distance between her and the man whose presence was swiftly filling the cabin.

"Joanna?" Fitzpaine said quietly.

A rush of something hot skimmed over Joanna's skin. *How dare he call her that!*

"I think I would prefer it," she said coldly, "if you called me Mrs. Epwin."

The man snorted. "Not a chance."

"H-How dare you!"

"You think I could get away with calling a woman who is supposed to be the Duchess of Fitzpaine 'Mrs. Epwin'?" the duke asked quietly. "You didn't think this through, did you?"

Joanna swallowed. *No. She had not.*

The trouble was, she was now going to have to live with the consequences.

Not forever, heaven's no. But a week trapped on this small ship with that man and a whole host of other men who believed them to be happily married?

It was going to feel like forever.

"I—" Joanna began.

She halted swiftly and thrust her hands to the wall as there was a sudden judder. Something snapped in the wind above them, the whole cabin moving.

"Ah, we've cast off," said the duke knowledgeably, stepping to one of the two chairs on either side of the door and seating himself on it comfortably. "Our journey begins."

Joanna tried not to meet his eye.

Yes, the journey begins. The trouble was, she had no idea how she was to survive it.

Deceit was not something in her character. Oh, she had lied to the duke about being married, but that had been self-preservation. That had been desperate. The man had a knife! This was something quite different.

"So, are you going to explain?"

Joanna's cheeks darkened at the amused expression on the

man's face. "Explain?"

Fitzpaine shrugged. "Not that I'm complaining, of course. But I am intrigued to hear why you thought this little charade was the best option."

"I think you will find it was the only option," Joanna managed to say.

Her mind whirled as she tried to consider what other choices there might have been. Was it possible she could have chosen a different route? Was there any other way to get them onto the *Liberté*?

"Only option?"

"It was obvious," Joanna said, words slipping from her mouth as her heart raced. "I would have thought a duke would have seen that."

It was an unguarded moment. Fitzpaine shifted in his chair. "It wasn't obvious to me," he said quietly.

Joanna swallowed.

Obvious was perhaps the wrong word, though she would not own that to a man like him. A man like Fitzpaine always got what he wanted. He had never had to consider if he was worthy. Never wondered if his father would permit him to do something as simple as stay at home reading a book rather than go to a dance.

The Duke of Fitzpaine, Joanna was sure, had never compromised in his entire life.

"You surprised me."

Joanna's cheeks flamed with a burning heat. "Yes. I did. I kissed you."

She caught Fitzpaine's eye. The contact only increased the scalding temperature rising.

Oh, such a kiss. Joanna had never kissed a man before. There had been no opportunity—no, that was not quite true. If she was honest with herself, there had been a few chances she had not taken, but they had all been with men for whom she felt no attraction.

Besides, her father would have been furious at the thought of his precious daughter and heiress kissing a man before they were engaged to be married, Joanna thought wretchedly.

Perhaps it was a good thing that he would never hear about this.

Whatever she had thought a kiss would be like, what she had shared with Fitzpaine had been different. Kissing was . . . well, it was a mechanical meeting of lips. Nothing more.

What she and Fitzpaine had experienced was far more. Heat, and desire, and longing. A sense of belonging. A feeling the world could fade away and it simply wouldn't matter. Joanna's gaze dropped to her hands. At least, that was how it had been for her. There was no knowing what the duke had felt.

This was ridiculous! She should not be thinking of that kiss—it had been a mistake. No, not a mistake. A means to an end. She had needed the captain to be convinced of their connection, and hopefully he had swallowed the bait.

Now all they had to do was live with each other. For a whole week.

"Joanna?"

Joanna's fingers curled on the wall, attempting to hold onto it as the ship gained pace. It was moving through the water far faster than the ship which had taken her to France. The swaying movement was playing havoc with her sense of balance.

Yes, it was that. Not Fitzpaine's presence.

"Joanna?" Fitzpaine repeated. There was something akin to tenderness in his voice.

Joanna swallowed and forced herself to look at him. They were about to spend a week—*a week!*—on this ship together. She would have to grow accustomed to looking at him. Her heart skipped a beat. If only he weren't so handsome. If only she couldn't remember so richly what it had felt for his hand to be on her waist—

"It was a kiss," Joanna said firmly, her voice weak. "Nothing more."

Fitzpaine raised a quizzical eyebrow. "I said nothing about

the kiss. You did."

Oh, bother.

"It was for a purpose," she said hastily, her shyness threatening to overwhelm. "I—I needed to convince—"

"I know why you did it, once you told him that ridiculous story about the two of us being married," Fitzpaine said quietly. "What I am still at a loss to understand is why you would spin that tale?"

Joanna hesitated. She barely knew herself, but that wasn't the sort of thing one could say to a man. Not even a gentleman. Especially not a duke.

"I did not wish to walk through France," she said quietly, testing the veracity of each word as she said it. "That would have taken weeks."

"It certainly would have done," Fitzpaine said dryly. "Particularly if you had not permitted me to ride on the horse."

Joanna tried not to smile. She had rather enjoyed forbidding him that. It had almost become a game, to see if she could inflict her will upon the duke who always got his own way.

"Precisely," she said aloud. "This way, we . . . we only have to put up with each other for a week."

A week had never seemed that long before. Joanna had let weeks drift by during her Seasons without ever attending a single event to which she'd been invited, much to the chagrin of her father.

"Why aren't you out there, dazzling the *ton*?" he would say.

And Joanna would flush, dissemble, try to explain to him she had no wish to dazzle.

"I just want the company of a few friends," Joanna had always said. "That is all."

"And I tell you, you will have no friends until you are wed!" her father had always thundered. "When you are married, then you can waste time with these friendships of yours!"

For a moment, just a moment, Joanna felt she was back there. Back in her childhood home, the tall townhouse in Camberley

Square, London. The place that was more prison than home.

She shut her eyes.

When she opened them again, she was standing in the cabin of the *Liberté*, and Fitzpaine was staring curiously.

"You disappeared there for a moment," he said conversationally. "It's not like my wife to ignore me."

Joanna swallowed the retort which a bolder woman would have made. *She was not his wife. And she never would be.*

"A week," Fitzpaine continued slowly. "So. We are going to have to put up with each other, as you say."

"If I'd had my way, I would be in my own cabin."

"So would I," he replied dryly. "Yet here we are. In *our* cabin."

It was all she could do not to look at the bed between them. The large bed. The bed that the captain had described as perfect for a married couple. If the kiss she had shared with Fitzpaine was anything to go by, then the thought of making love in—

Joanna staggered to the left as her mind rebelled against the rush of images flooding her mind. Of her and the duke. Of clothes gone and kisses descending . . .

She was not going to lose her head!

"I suppose we are just going to have to cope," said Joanna firmly, more to herself than the duke who appeared to be unperturbed. "If we are careful, no one on the ship will ever suspect we are—"

"Almost strangers," said Fitzpaine softly.

Joanna's heart skipped a beat. She wasn't certain anyone she had kissed so heartily could be described as a stranger.

"Exactly," she lied. "After all, it's only seven days."

And seven nights. The words were not spoken by either of them, but Joanna could hear them echoing around the room. Around the bed which she tried, again, not to look at.

"We'll be in England before you know it!" Joanna tried to say brightly.

The ship suddenly lurched to one side but this time she kept her balance.

If only she could keep that same equilibrium around the handsome man staring at her with a strange expression. Almost as though he distrusted her.

Her? He was the one who had abducted her at knife point!

"You'll have to practice."

Joanna did not look around. "Practice?"

"You are no duchess, Mrs. Epwin, if you do not mind me saying," said the duke haughtily. "You will have to practice."

"Practice?" That had caught her attention.

Practice being a duchess? She had never heard of a more ridiculous thing!

Except that he was right, of course. The last thing they needed was someone guessing that she was not truly a duchess. Why, the scandal!

"It's easy once you get the hang of it," said the duke nonchalantly. "Anyone could pretend to be a duke or a duchess as long as they had enough confidence."

Joanna almost laughed. Confidence? It was not a character strength of hers. More a flaw. "I . . . I will do my best."

"You know, if I did not know any better," Fitzpaine said quietly. "If I did not already know you were wed, I would have said this was a ploy for my hand. An attempt at seduction. A hope the pretense of being a duchess for this week would become something permanent."

Joanna's mouth fell open. Though it had never been her intention to entrap the man, she could not disagree it may look like that. If she had not lied, that was.

Oh, goodness. This was getting complicated. Joanna had never been one for Society's intrigues. Oh, she read about them in the gossip pages of course. There was nothing better than living vicariously through the lives of other people. As long as her name was not mentioned in them, her father had always said, then she was permitted to read them. Maybe he thought that would encourage her to attend Almack's more often. It had never worked.

"Well, that is not a problem," Joanna managed to say coolly. "For I am married, and I have absolutely no intention of—of seducing you."

Her cheeks burned as she said the words and a smile teased on Fitzpaine's lips.

"No, I suppose it would not occur to you," he said softly. "Except for that kiss. I could believe almost anything of you now that I've tasted your lips."

Joanna's chest tightened but somehow she was unable to look away. *That he could say such a thing! And to a married woman, too!*

Well. What he thought was a married woman.

"H-How dare you!" she spluttered. "I have no intention of—"

"You truly wish to tell me you would never do such a thing?" Fitzpaine said darkly. He had risen to his feet. "You believe yourself so virtuous that if you were not married, Mrs. Epwin, you would not wish to land me? That you and your family would not be pleased to have hooked a duke?"

Joanna swallowed and tried not to think of what her father would say if she returned to England a duchess.

Because Fitzpaine was right. She may loathe that he was, but he was. And if he knew the truth—that she had lied about being married, and was innocent . . .

That he was her first kiss.

Joanna flushed. "I said I would never do such a thing, and I meant it."

"Oh, I think you'll find that for most ladies, where there's a duke, there's a way to convince themselves of the morality of their actions," Fitzpaine said darkly. "I don't know what your true intentions are, Joanna—"

"I told you—"

"You are an enigma," he said flatly. "A woman I cannot understand, and I will not be part of your games, Mrs. Epwin. Not today. Not ever."

And before Joanna could say a word, the duke had stormed from the cabin and left her in silence.

Chapter Seven

7 February, 1811

ARTHUR HAD LAIN awake for what felt like forever.

It had been a compromise. *Hopefully the treaty to end this war with France would be negotiated with less intensity*, he had thought bitterly as Joanna clearly marked along the middle of the large bed precisely which was his half, and which was hers.

"It's not like we have another choice," she had said, puritanically averting her gaze as she got into bed. "There's not even a chaise longue here for you to lie on."

Arthur had refrained from arguing that since he was a duke, he had the higher rank and deserved a whole bed, even if she was a lady. Then he wondered if, because he was a duke, he needed to be gallant, or chivalrous, or something else they taught at Eton. But as there hadn't been another choice—or a chaise longue—it had seemed churlish to argue.

And so they had gone to bed. The same bed. Joanna had slipped off to sleep almost immediately, her slow breathing gentle as Arthur had stared at the ceiling.

Lying by a woman who was so beautiful and wearing naught but a nightgown—apparently the captain's wife had been all too eager to lend her one when she heard the Duchess of Fitzpaine had lost all her luggage—was sadly not particularly conducive to sleep.

Arthur had been painfully conscious of the woman beside him the entire night. Her warmth. The way she snuffled slightly in her sleep as she turned over. The tantalizingly small space between them that could be breached at any moment, line in bed linens be damned.

Whatever sleep he had managed to get, it had been broken. By the time daylight started to slowly drift through the cracks around the curtain, Arthur was certain he had managed only an hour or two of sleep.

He probably looked more tired leaving the cabin than he had when he had entered. But he had left, nonetheless. He could not stand it any longer.

Arthur carefully tried to close the door without too much noise. Joanna had barely stirred as he had risen and hastily dressed. She must have been exhausted.

For a moment, sympathy washed through him. She was a lady, after all—a true lady, more gentility in her little finger than he had in his whole body. Even if she did not know it.

Kidnapped by the French in Paris, dragged down to the south for goodness knows how long, then taken by him—yes, fine, at knife point, though he would not have hurt her. No wonder she was sleeping so soundly.

Arthur glanced one way then the other along the gently shifting corridor. Now, which way was it up to the deck? He thought it was—

"Ah, Your Grace!"

Arthur started. He had not noticed the captain suddenly appear at his side. "Hush!"

Captain Toussaint frowned. "I beg your pardon?"

Arthur jerked his head to the door. "Joanna—my wife, I mean. She's still asleep."

My wife. The words were hollow. They tasted strange in his mouth.

He had not said them aloud since they had boarded the ship. Last night had been such a fiasco, he had eaten in the dining hall in a temper. It had only been halfway through the meal that he had realized Joanna had not eaten.

It had been easy enough to get a man to send a tray down. She had thanked him when he had returned, finally so exhausted he could think of nowhere else to go. Her gratitude had only increased his guilt.

"Ah, the duchess still slumbers," nodded Captain Toussaint with a knowing look. "I can imagine after the night you gave her—"

"Yes, thank you," Arthur said hastily.

He was not embarrassed. *He was not!*

Well, perhaps a little. He was hardly a saint, but the idea of any woman being spoken of like that by a stranger. A Frenchman! And he thought her a duchess!

"I was going up for a bit of fresh air," Arthur said, stepping away from the door, hoping they had not disturbed Joanna.

The instinct surprised him. Since when did he care if he was disturbing Joanna or not?

It was that damned kiss. It was starting to play havoc with him.

"I understand—that way," said the captain, pointing to Arthur's left.

"Good morning."

"Good—"

He did not wait for the captain to finish. For the first time since he had started pretending to be someone of great birth and nobility, Arthur was starting to get tired of all this.

The bowing, the scraping. He had never thought to grow weary of such civilities, but after being cooped up on the *Liberté* for not even a day it was starting to grate. What was coming over him?

Arthur took a deep breath of fresh salty air as he reached the deck. *Ah, that was better.* The brilliant sunshine was not warm, but it was bright. It awakened him far more than anything else, including a conversation with the captain, ever could.

The balustrade was not elegantly carved, but it was solid. Arthur grasped it, fingers curling around the heavy wood. In all the confusion and change and surprises Joanna had given him, it was reassuring to hold something which could not slip from his fingertips.

For a few minutes, Arthur merely watched the waves. The shoreline of France was just visible through the morning's haze, but he instead chose to look out to sea. The waves rocked the ship, the gentle rhythm soothing him much as he expected a lullaby would.

In less than a week, he would be in England again.

It was a strange thought. Arthur had never thought he would return to England. There had been nothing to return to, but there was even less in France if Laurent's truth got out.

No, eventually the jig would be up. Someone would realize there was no dukedom of Fitzpaine, or he would do something like eat an escargot with the wrong fork—heaven forbid. Laurent would be believed by someone, and the ruse would come tumbling down.

Better to get out while he was ahead, Arthur told himself firmly. He had some money left from his adventures. Not much, but enough to get up north. Perhaps he could visit a baronet, spin the same tale. If he were offered hospitality there, he could spend the rest of the winter lying low before deciding what to do next. Perhaps—

"Hie there!"

Arthur started, dragged unexpectedly from his reverie by a cry. He turned, heart pounding. *That did not sound good.*

When his eyes caught up with his senses, he could swiftly see that it wasn't. A sailor had slipped his footing in the tall rigging encircling the mast and was falling.

Falling—to the deck, where he would surely be greatly injured. Killed.

Arthur did not think. Thinking took time, and he had always run on instinct.

Lurching forward and running as fast as he could, boots almost slipping on the wave-damp decking, Arthur held out his hands as the man tumbled faster and faster down.

"Together!"

A sailor had yelled as he rushed toward Arthur, arms similarly outstretched. They interlocked hands, stepping quickly together just as the sailor fell into their waiting arms.

Arthur groaned. The sudden falling weight of the man wrenched at his shoulders, but they were able to slow the man's fall.

The three of them collapsed.

"Pierre!"

"Dear God, is he well?"

"Who is that, that saved him?"

A medley of noises, of voices. Arthur's vision was sparkling with lights popping in all directions. *Stars. Stars? It couldn't be stars, it was daylight.*

After blinking frantically, his heart still pounding, Arthur's eyesight slowly returned.

He was lying on the deck of the ship. His side was damp from lying on the wet planks, his arms aching painfully from the sudden lurch they had suffered in his attempt to catch the falling man. His hands hurt. His shoulders were heaving.

And a French sailor was looking at him blearily.

"You saved me, monsieur," he gasped.

Arthur nodded, hardly knowing what he was doing. "I suppose I did."

"That's no monsieur!" came a voice a long way away, but Arthur recognized with a sinking heart as Captain Toussaint. "That's the Duke of Fitzpaine!"

Gasps resounded as Arthur pushed himself on his elbows and looked around him.

Ah. It appeared every single sailor on the *Liberté,* and every passenger, was on the deck. They were all staring. Slowly, one by one, they all began to do something that made Arthur feel more mortified than he had ever felt in his life.

They were applauding. *Oh, God, no.*

"That will be something to tell your grandchildren, Pierre," someone was saying gleefully in rustic French. "Saved from death by a duke!"

"I did not know dukes could run that fast!" someone else said. "Did you see?"

Arthur wished to goodness they would all stop staring.

Hell's bells. The last thing he wanted was to draw more attention to himself. He had hoped to just sail along to England, slip off the ship without having any awkward conversations, and disappear into the crowds.

"What a hero," a woman who could have been the captain's wife was saying.

Arthur's smile grew more brittle. And the worst of it was, the one person he wished could have witnessed his miraculous rescue wasn't even here.

Joanna.

Though he could try to pretend he did not care what she thought of him, Arthur had to admit if he could impress one person on this ship, it would be Joanna. But she was not here. She had not witnessed this great moment.

Which was a good thing, Arthur told himself as he wordlessly shook hands with Pierre and the other sailor who had helped to rescue him, then stepped away from the crowd. The last thing he needed was to get even more entangled with that woman.

Joanna Epwin was married. Married. She had a husband!

Which was precisely why he should not be already looking forward to the evening. The chance for him to once again clamber into bed beside her . . .

His fingers grasped the balustrade once more as he took a deep breath. *Well, she had not seen. That was that.*

"That was brave," said a quiet voice.

Arthur's heart skipped a beat. He knew that voice.

Whirling around on the balls of his feet, he saw Joanna. She was standing behind him in that blue gown—the only gown, now he came to think of it, she owned.

His stomach lurched. *Brave? She thought he was brave?*

Joy, ridiculous joy, leapt within him. She had seen it! Joanna had witnessed his sudden rush to save a man. In that moment, it all became worth the ache in his joints.

The joy faded as guilt replaced it. What sort of a cad was he, who could only find happiness in a man's life being saved if it brought him benefit?

"It was nothing," Arthur said stiffly, turning back to the balustrade.

Yes, that was the right thing to do. If he spoke curtly she would go away, and he could be left to wrestle with his conscience in peace.

Joanna's small hands clasped the balustrade just inches from his own. "No, it wasn't nothing. You saved a man's life."

Arthur tried not to puff out his chest. This was not a moment for preening. If he were a true duke, he would be honest. He would explain it was instincts only, and he would not have been successful if it had not been for that other fellow. And a whole heap of luck.

But he wasn't a duke.

"His life was saved," Arthur conceded, a compromise between his conscience and his desire to impress. "Is that not enough?"

"It is still impressive," Joanna said softly.

He glanced at her, then wished he hadn't. She was looking out to sea, eyes brilliantly blue. Had they always been that color? Or were they merely reflecting the sea?

Arthur tried to think of something to say, but all his words were fleeing his mind. How did people do this, anyway? Converse lightly with someone who had kissed you most heartily the day before?

All of his previous liaisons, for want of a better word, had been clean cut. He knew what they wanted, they knew what he wanted, and once the evening was over, they slipped into the night, never to be seen again. It was easier that way.

Joanna sighed. "I am sorry."

Arthur blinked. "Sorry?"

What on earth could the woman be sorry for?

She turned, arm brushing against his own, and smiled ruefully. "For pretending to Captain Toussaint that we are man and wife."

Arthur jerked his head over his shoulder. It did not appear that there was anyone close enough to think to overhear. Thank God. "It's nothing."

"No, you were quite within your right to chastise me yesterday," Joanna said in a rush. "It was just, I could think of no other alternative, and the moment I thought—"

"You acted," Arthur said dryly. He had to admit, he was in awe of the woman. "Despite being shy. Despite hating attention. Despite always wishing to pass through the world without anyone taking a second glance at you."

Joanna's lips parted as her eyes widened in amazement. "How did you know—"

"This may come as a surprise to you, but I know you better than you think," Arthur said gently. "You are a shy woman, Joanna. That is nothing to be ashamed of."

For some reason, though, she was. Her cheeks blushed as she looked away.

"Perhaps not for a duke," she said softly. "But my—most people in my life believe me to be too reticent."

"I certainly wouldn't call you that," Arthur said without thinking, the memory of her hand around his neck too potent to ignore.

He had embarrassed her. Yet she did not leave his presence, as he had expected. Joanna just stood beside him as the ocean breeze rustled her curls.

They stood for a minute or two in silence, and Arthur was astonished to find he enjoyed it. He was not usually one for silence. Silence lasting too long usually meant something bad was about to happen. His habit of always filling a quiet moment in a conversation, however, was quelled. Standing here with Joanna in silence was . . . enough. Her presence was enough.

"Still," she said softly. "I am sorry. You did not wish to spend this voyage with a pretend duchess by your side."

Arthur swallowed the jest that it was appropriate, as he was a pretend duke.

No, the moment to confess had passed long ago. He would simply have to learn to live with the lie a little longer.

He tried to grin as the ship rocked. "I just feel guilty for your true husband, that's all. I imagine he never thought he would have to share you."

A strange look, something he had never seen before, flickered across Joanna's face. It wasn't guilt, but it wasn't far off. It was great discomfort, and a stoical firmness. It was most odd. If the expression had lasted longer, Arthur would have been pleased to study it. But it flickered away much like a wave disappeared onto the shore.

"Yes," she said stiffly. "My husband."

"I suppose you were separated in Paris," Arthur said, hating the man even existed but finding it impossible not to ask about him. "What is his name?"

As he watched Joanna war within herself, evidently unhappy about discussing her true husband with her false one, Arthur had a battle of his own to fight.

He was not jealous. Well, perhaps just a tad. It was hard not to be, now he had tasted the sweet lips of the woman beside him.

Joanna was something different. Not one of these flashy ladies of the *ton*, interested in nothing more than being admired. No, she was more refined. More delicate. A lesser man would mistake it for primness. He had, at first. But it was shyness and, entwined with that, a sort of passion only released when she had kissed him.

Arthur shifted his feet awkwardly as he tried not to relieve that moment again. Such passion, yet such restraint.

"His name—his name is Tom."

Arthur blinked. "Tom?"

Joanna nodded. "Yes, Tom. That's . . . he is . . . we were not married long."

Ah. Well, that would explain it. There was a nervousness this woman had around men Arthur would never have expected in a wife. But if they had only married recently—and though she had given him no firm evidence, Arthur was certain . . .

Well, it happened all the time, didn't it, with the nobility and gentry? Arthur had heard of it countless times—an arranged marriage. Was that why she was so hesitant to speak of her husband? Was the truth that Joanna knew very little about the man she had so recently married?

"I am sorry that the two of you were ripped apart so swiftly," was all he managed to say.

For some reason, Joanna did not look particularly sorry about it. She shrugged in the bracing air. "I . . . well. When it happened, when the French came—barreling up the stairs of the hotels, shouts, and screams, I knew something terrible was going to happen. Something I would be unable to escape."

He moved unconsciously closer to her. There was pain in her words, and fear. Fear that, as a man with his wits about him and an elementary knowledge of boxing, he had never known. Arthur had never found himself in a situation where he could not defend himself.

"I thought, for a while, they would just keep me for a few days as a prize," Joanna was continuing, looking out to see. "But days, weeks went by. I lost all track of time. I kept thinking about that moment when they pulled me from my bed, laughing, jeering . . ."

Her voice trailed away.

Arthur swallowed. Dear God, he'd never thought about it.

She must have been terrified, lived in terror for months. No wonder she had been so sharp with him when he'd pulled a knife on her and dragged her into the darkness on a horse.

"Thankfully they never touched me—not . . . not like that." It was clearly difficult for her to keep going, but she continued, "I was kept almost like an oddity. An officer provided a room for me wherever the camp went, and I was fed, mostly, and just . . . kept. Waiting. Waiting to discover what they would do with me."

"And your husband?"

He had not intended to ask the question, but it slipped from his lips before he could stop it.

Joanna breathed out slowly. "I . . . I don't know."

Hell's bells. He needed to change the tone of the conversation swiftly, or else he may find himself truly caring for this woman and her plight.

"Well, you found someone," Arthur said bracingly. "Plenty of people do not find anyone, Jojo."

"Jojo?"

Heat tinged his cheeks as he looked at the woman beside him, flushing just as deeply as he was sure he was.

"It was a slip of the tongue," he said defensively. "I apologize, I—"

"No, I rather like it," said Joanna with a nervous smile. "I . . . well. I never had a friend to give me a nickname before. I like that it was a duke who gave me my first. My first nickname. My first kiss."

Possessive desire rose in Arthur as he tried to digest her words.

God, he was in danger here. Joanna Epwin, no matter what she might think of herself, was a tasty morsel of a woman who would have been snapped up by any sensible man the moment he saw her.

Arthur certainly knew what he wanted to do with her.

Yet she was someone else's wife, he had to remember that. This Tom.

Pushing aside his bitter jealousy of the man who was permitted to touch, to tease, and be with Jojo, Arthur tried once again to smile. "It's hard to make your way in the world without someone by your side. You have Tom. That's . . . that's good."

And much to his surprise, Jojo looked wistful. "Yes. Something like that."

CHAPTER EIGHT

"—AND OF COURSE, you must dine at my table!"

Jojo tried to smile.

Strange, how swiftly she started to consider herself "Jojo". Arthur—*the Duke of Fitzpaine*, she reminded herself sternly—had only called her that for the first time hours ago.

Yet it had slipped into her soul. It had become her. It was a part of her now, and whenever she saw his determined gaze drifting toward her, Jojo discovered to her surprise that she wanted to hear him call her that again. Just one more time.

"Well, you found someone. Plenty of people do not find anyone, Jojo."

"Jojo?"

She shivered. The night air had crept even below the deck, and the only gown she had was not designed for the winter climes.

It had been foolish, really, to bring it to Paris in the first place. She had never expected, however, to be abducted while wearing it.

"Dine at your table?" Fitzpaine repeated, catching Jojo's eye. "Ah. What an honor."

Jojo did her best to incline her head gracefully to the beaming Captain Toussaint. "What an honor indeed."

And it was supposed to be, she knew. Though she had never

been on a ship like this before—the crossing to France had taken but a few hours—Jojo had a good enough idea of ship etiquette to know dining at the captain's table was a privilege.

The only trouble was, it would force her and Fitzpaine to keep up the pretense of their marriage even longer into the evening than they had expected. Or hoped.

"Or we could sit on one of the other tables, over there," said Fitzpaine, gesturing as they entered the dining hall.

Jojo suppressed a smile. A table as far from the captain's as it was possible to be.

"Nonsense!" roared Captain Toussaint, unwilling to take no for an answer. "I have never had such distinguished passengers on my ship. A duke and a duchess! A hero!"

Jojo glanced at her pretend husband and saw the great discomfort on the man's face. Most men, as far as she was aware, would adore to be considered a hero. They would want to be feted for even the smallest thing. But Fitzpaine?

He looked in agony every time someone mentioned it.

"Well," the duke said helplessly, glancing at Jojo as though for help.

Jojo's cheeks burned. *What was she supposed to say?* "How delightful."

She saw the flicker of disappointment in her false husband's eyes and dropped her gaze. She'd known it would happen. He would expect something from her, something bold, brash, brilliant. And she would disappoint.

Anyone who knew her, Jojo thought bitterly, would know not to ask anything of her. She was not that sort of woman. Shyness was not a crime, as far as she was concerned. But it may as well be in polite Society.

"Here, let me pull out a chair, Your Grace," said the captain, hastily rushing over to the long table that headed the dining hall.

Jojo looked at Fitzpaine for help.

He grinned. "How *delightful.*"

It was all she could do not to roll her eyes as she stepped

across the dining hall and sat on the waiting chair pulled out by the captain. *How dare Fitzpaine use her own words against her! It was outrageous!*

Jojo tried not to notice the eyes flickering to herself and the man seated beside her.

Well, she had once been curious to look at a duke. The last time she and Fitzpaine had sat at a dining table, after all, had been with those horrendous French captains, and she had spent most of the meal not eating, but sneaking glances at the handsome man beside her.

Little had she known then she would have plenty of opportunity to look at him later.

"I just hope our simple fare will be sufficient for such noble—"

"I am sure whatever you have will be fine," said Fitzpaine curtly.

Jojo glanced over, just for a moment.

That was another odd thing about the Duke of Fitzpaine. She had met dukes before. The *ton* appeared to be inundated with them. One could barely move at Almack's for stepping on a duke's toes. And they had been . . . different from him.

Oh, they had been just as haughty. And just as handsome. In some cases, Fitzpaine was far more so.

But this duke was—she couldn't understand it. Less comfortable with others. Less accustomed, it seemed, to being looked at, watched, stared at.

Now, Jojo could well understand his dislike of the attention. She would hate to be so observed at all times. But it was almost as though Fitzpaine was not used to it, which made no sense. The man had to be at least as old as her, must have spent years in Society. So why—

"Ah, the escargot," Captain Toussaint said, rubbing his hands.

Fitzpaine's groan was slight. Jojo was certain she had been the only one to hear it.

She forced her lips to curve into a smile. "Ah, a French delicacy."

"Only the best for the Duke and Duchess of Fitzpaine!"

"But they don't have snails," pointed out the duke, gesturing at the other guests.

Jojo looked up from her steaming plate of shells.

"Oh, I have given them a paltry portion of roast chicken," said Captain Toussaint, waving a hand dismissively. "I would not insult you by serving you such peasant food!"

Jojo's gaze flickered to the man beside her and saw the hunger. *Well, if there was ever a moment to be bold.*

"I have heard, Captain," she said timidly, trying to give her voice a little more power. "I have heard the French roast their chickens in a far superior way to the English."

As expected, the man's chest swelled. "I have not heard that, Your Grace, but I would not be surprised! The French, as I am sure you are now aware, are superior in all—"

"It would be a shame if my husband and I were not able to sample the roast chicken—to compare, I mean," Jojo said, lowering her voice and trembling slightly at being so forward. "Otherwise, we will not be able to tell people in England, you see."

For a moment, just a moment, she caught Fitzpaine's eye.

She had to immediately look away. There was such a look of amazement she was certain she would blush and the captain would become suspicious.

"Bring two more roast chickens!" roared the captain, waving at one of the crew.

The man blinked. "Two—two whole chickens?"

"Only the very best for our honored guests," came the thunderous response.

As the two sailors argued, Fitzpaine leaned close to Jojo. "That was brilliant."

"That was desperate," Jojo said, trying to smile and ignoring the heat rushing through her the closer the duke grew. "I couldn't eat the snails either."

She almost heard Fitzpaine moan aloud as two roast chickens

were placed before them. They did smell good. Rosemary and butter and—

"Only the very best," repeated the captain genially. "For my honored guests."

For the next ten minutes or so, conversation was impossible. *At least, it could have occurred*, Jojo thought wryly, *but it would have been remarkably one sided.*

It was not as though she and the duke had been starved on their journey. The inn had provided a good enough meal, and the breakfast on the ship was passable. But there was nothing like hearty food like roast chicken to fill a person with delight. Especially when the alternative had threatened to be snails.

"So, tell me," said Captain Toussaint. "How did you wed? Was it an arranged marriage?"

Jojo looked up hastily. Fitzpaine's hand, holding a fork, had frozen halfway to his mouth. *An arranged marriage?*

This was precisely what she had been afraid of, yet done nothing about. Why had they not agreed a story between them, so that if this situation were to occur they would know what to say?

"Oh, it's not a very interesting story," said Fitzpaine dismissively, not looking at her.

A flush tinged Jojo's cheeks. Even when it was a false marriage, her "husband" had no interest in discussing her. She was just that dull.

But it appeared the captain, once again, would not take no for an answer. "Come, I would greatly enjoy being entertained! It is rare that I have a duke here to ask such questions, and I hope you do not think me impertinent, my lady."

Jojo swallowed her mouthful of chicken and looked fearfully at Fitzpaine. He refused to look at her, staring at his chicken.

And something strange rose in Jojo which she had never felt before. It was not boldness; one did not change from being shy overnight, it simply was not possible.

But a . . . a playfulness rose, something teasing and joyful as she looked at Fitzpaine's profile. He was so handsome, and he could do nothing but pretend to be her husband for the week that they were on this ship.

Then why not have a little fun?

"You could say Fitzpaine swept me off my feet," Jojo said slowly. "Didn't you, darling?"

Fitzpaine stiffened, then turned and lowered his mouth to her ear. "Just what do you think you are doing?"

Jojo shivered, the warmth of his breath doing something strange as it blossomed over her skin. "I'm—"

"Swept you off your feet!" crowed the captain. "Oh, I do enjoy a romantic. Your Grace, I had no idea you had it in you!"

"Neither did I," said Fitzpaine stiffly as he straightened, a glare still remaining.

But the playfulness that had arisen within her could not be so easily dampened. After years of always being on the sidelines, always being ignored, never witty enough, clever enough, charming enough, Jojo had finally had enough.

"Yes, he swept me off my feet," she said, remembering how rapidly Fitzpaine had pulled her from the French captain's table and thrust the knife close. "Quite against my better judgment, wasn't it, Fitzpaine?"

When he met her gaze, Jojo could see he was remembering the same moment. Almost despite himself it appeared, a wry smile tweaked his lips.

"Something like that," he said gruffly.

"Before a whole host of other men," Jojo continued, smiling shyly at the captain as her story unfolded. "I think many of them were quite surprised that you did so, weren't they?"

Fitzpaine was almost grinning now, and it did something wonderful to Jojo's stomach, filling it with soaring warmth.

"They did look startled, yes," he owned. A gleam of mischief sparkled in his eye. "I believe I then took you riding, isn't that right?"

"Rather forcibly, I seem to remember," Jojo shot back.

Oh, this was wonderful! Was this what it was to be witty? Was this what other women felt like all the time? As though every word that poured from their mouths was going to be received well, perhaps even adored?

Jojo could feel her heart pattering, faster and faster, but unlike every other time in her life, this was not the rapid heartbeat of panic. No, this was . . . wonderful. Enjoyable.

"I seem to remember you didn't like walking," quipped Fitzpaine with a laugh. "You were the one who insisted on riding."

Jojo laughed and he laughed with her, and it was as though the captain, the ship, all the crew and other passengers, had disappeared. This was a moment between the two of them, herself and the duke.

A sense of wild abandon was flooding through her. Was it possible that life and laughter were this easy for some? That words were just there, ready and waiting on the tip of the tongue, which could elicit such joy in others?

It was like . . . like a fizzing of the blood. As though every inch of her was on fire, but it was a warm, gentle flame.

Jojo caught Fitzpaine's eye. *Perhaps not gentle.*

"We've had interesting times," Fitzpaine was saying, more to the captain than her.

Jojo was grateful. She was not certain she could maintain this . . . well, what was it? Flirtation?

Shame flickered through her heart. Her father would certainly not approve of such behavior. He would consider it wanton, unseemly. Unacceptable. But it wasn't just flirtation that Jojo was feeling. It was something more. Something delightful, something akin to . . .

Affection?

Jojo looked at her almost empty plate. *She was being ridiculous.* She had told him she was already married! Any hope that this could grow into anything like affection was wasted. That door was closed. She had locked it before she had even realized she may wish to step through it.

"—very beautiful, of course," she overheard the captain saying.

Heat scalded her cheeks, and Jojo wished to goodness she had not been paying attention at that very moment. The last thing she wanted to do was hear Fitzpaine deny—

"Oh yes, she's a beauty," the duke said softly. "Sometimes I wonder if she knows it."

Jojo's fingers tangled into a rather complicated knot in her lap. She had mistaken them. They could not be speaking of her, that was simply not possible.

When she glanced up, both men were looking at her. Both men smiled.

With her lungs tightening, and wondering how she would ever look them or anyone else in the eye again, Jojo dropped her gaze. She had never thought Fitzpaine considered her that way. Their interactions had been stiff at best, prim and distant at worst. He had never—there had been no mention of—

And the affection which had swelled during their flirtatious back and forth, as they gave the captain a rather clever explanation of how they had met, blossomed once more.

Was it possible Fitzpaine felt the same?

Jojo knew she was being ridiculous. The clatter of the dining hall was growing as people became more raucous, and she was relieved the attention of the room appeared to have shifted to a sailor who had brought out a fiddle.

". . . yes, rather special . . ."

Jojo closed her eyes for a moment, then forced them open. *Fitzpaine's words were for show*, she told herself sternly. The whole ship thought they were married. It was entirely natural for him to speak about her like that!

Unless he was starting to do what Lady Romeril had once sternly reprimanded her not to do: "catch feelings."

"Young ladies these days seem to catch feelings no matter where they go, or what the gentleman has offered," Lady Romeril had said sharply to Jojo just days before she had left for Paris. "I am glad to see that you, my dear, do nothing of the sort. Why, you do not even flirt with the young men! A woman to be proud of."

Jojo had felt shame in that moment. Lady Romeril could not have made it plainer that she was indeed plain. That no gentleman had bothered to look at her, and so she had been afforded no opportunities to "catch feelings," as she put it.

Well, she was catching them now.

Jojo caught Fitzpaine's eye. Warmth suffused through her, the tension lessening its pressure. Yet her heart was still beating frantically. Was this all teasing from him, or could it be something more?

"And you must have had your pick of the ladies, Your Grace, a duke like yourself," Captain Toussaint said impressively, evidently hoping to charm.

Jojo's heart sank.

"Oh, I—I wouldn't say that," dissembled Fitzpaine with a laugh.

Her heart sank even lower. *Of course he wouldn't. He did not need to.*

The man was a duke. A handsome duke. What woman could resist? *The poor thing probably had ladies throwing themselves at him all the time,* Jojo thought dully. He was probably bored of it.

All the playfulness shriveled up. Her gumption, as her father would have called it, disappeared. Her gaze dulled as Jojo ceased paying attention to conversations around her.

Fitzpaine was a duke, and a man who had been outraged that she had pretended to be his wife. She would truly be lying to herself if she believed it possible he could find her as charming and engaging as any of the ladies he had undoubtedly left behind.

"—must go and pay some attention to my other passengers," Captain Toussaint's voice cut through her thoughts. "Please do excuse me, Your Graces."

"Not at all," said Fitzpaine lightly.

Jojo was aware of the captain leaving their table, his chair pushed back and his heavy footsteps disappearing into the noise of the room.

They would be able to retire to their cabin soon, and there they could sit in silence until it was time, Jojo thought as her stomach lurched, *for bed.* Another night she would share a bed with a duke.

"I didn't know," Fitzpaine said quietly, leaning close, "you could laugh like that."

Jojo's cheeks and neck flushed with heat. It was all she could do to lift her gaze to his, and when she did, she gasped.

There was such interest. Such curiosity. She'd never seen him look like that before.

"I only laugh when I'm happy," Jojo said defensively. "I'm not like other women."

Fitzpaine raised an eyebrow. "Other women?"

Oh, why did she have to go and catch feelings for a man like this! One who only sought to tease her, one who was a duke—one who thought her already married!

"In Society," Jojo said, hating every word she said. "They laugh at anything anyone says to them. They do it to impress and I—I am not like them."

It had been one of her father's greatest criticisms. Why could she not just laugh at what gentlemen said? She'd be married within a month!

But Fitzpaine did not frown. He did not look disappointed, or irritated, or shake his head with disbelief.

Instead, he nodded. "Yes," he said softly, his gaze raking over her face. "Not like them—other women. I am starting to understand that."

CHAPTER NINE

"*Y*ES. *NOT LIKE them—other women. I am starting to understand that.*"

Arthur did everything he could to keep his face calm, though he wished immediately to ask further questions of this enigmatic woman.

How did she do it? Surprise him with her flirtation, then immediately disappear into the quiet shy woman he had thought she was. Challenge him with her gaze, tell him directly she was not like any of the sycophantic women he had been harassed by whenever they "discovered" he was a duke, then return to her shell?

She was maddening!

"Jojo," Arthur said quietly.

He saw the smile as she heard the nickname he had accidentally given her. How on earth was he going to disentangle himself from her when they arrived in England? He would have to see that she was well, naturally. Help her find her husband?

Arthur's heart rebelled against the very thought. *Perhaps not.*

"You . . . you look nice," he said lamely.

The instant the words left his mouth, Arthur knew he would spontaneously combust with embarrassment.

Nice? Nice? Was that all he could say to the woman who had been drawing everyone's attention for the last hour?

"Oh," Jojo said faintly. "Right. Thank you, I suppose."

Arthur almost groaned. *This was ridiculous.* He was hardly a green-gilled boy of eighteen, attending his first dinner and finding himself next to a beauty! He was a man of near thirty. He had charmed women before. In fact, one of the easiest ways to get through the world, he had swiftly found, was by charming ladies. So much easier that way.

So why was he having such difficulty saying anything pleasant to this woman, who was far more charming, far more elegant—

And far less available, a dark voice whispered in his mind.

Arthur's jaw tightened, but he could not deny it. Joanna Epwin was married. She was a wife already—and not his. There was a man somewhere out there who had a greater claim on her than anything Arthur could dream of. Soon, within a week, he would have to cede whatever fanciful ideas he had on Jojo's person and return her to the man who had already made her his wife.

Arthur swallowed. "Jojo—"

"Yes?" she said swiftly, her large blue eyes meeting his.

His words fell away. What on earth was happening to him? What was this tightness in his chest, this itch in his fingers? How was he supposed to talk if his mouth would not obey?

Arthur cleared his throat sternly. This was preposterous. He was a duke!

Well. Not exactly. But everyone on this ship, including Jojo, believed. Time he started acting like it.

"I was thinking," he began.

"Dancing!"

Cheers went up throughout the dining hall at Captain Toussaint's suggestion.

Arthur groaned as Jojo's gaze darted to the captain standing on the other side of the room. *Not dancing. Please, anything but—*

"I thought it would be pleasant to give our honored guests a little entertainment!" the captain was saying, to the general applause of the other passengers. "We have an excellent fiddler player in young Pierre, and—"

Arthur rose to his feet.

"Fitzpaine? Where are you going?" came the breathless voice.

"I am returning to the cabin," said Arthur sharply—far more sharply than he intended.

Jojo's gaze flickered, then drifted away. "I see."

No, she didn't see. Of course she didn't. She believed him to be a duke, born and raised. A duke, moreover, who would have had extensive experience in the art of dancing. An art that in his case was more like a disaster.

"There is no possibility of convincing me to dance," Arthur said in an undertone.

"Why?"

He almost cursed aloud at the innocent question. It wasn't just the single word. It was the way she asked it. Wide eyed, curious, innocent. She would believe anything he told her—Arthur could see that. Anything at all.

Dear God, it was a good thing she was already married. Arthur knew he could charm almost any woman, and Jojo Epwin was proving to be a most enticing prospect.

"And I see His Grace is eager to begin!" called over Captain Toussaint with a laugh. "Thank you, Your Grace. Will you lead us in the dancing?"

Arthur's hand gripped the back of his chair as he saw the Captain of the *Liberté* had entirely misunderstood him. He had not risen because he was eager to start dancing. He was about to leave this dining hall completely.

"Thank you, Your Grace, for honoring us by leading the first dance," a passenger that Arthur had never spoken to before called out.

This was madness! And it had gone far enough.

"I am sorry to disappoint you all," Arthur said, hating speaking in French. "But I am very tired, I had actually risen to return to my—our cabin."

Cries went out in disappointment, but he did not heed them. Instead, he was looking at Jojo with a beseeching expression.

"Please, Jojo," Arthur said softly. "Please, come with me."

Jojo immediately rose. "Of course, we—"

"See, your wife is eager to dance!" the captain's wife cried. "Remind me to lend you a few gowns my dear. Come, dance!"

Panic was growing in Arthur's chest, but he could not think how to stop this. The whole room was nodding, eagerly awaiting the first dance. A dance he was supposed to lead.

How on earth did one dance in such a space, anyway? Arthur started to feel the walls closing in. There was no escape, no possibility of reprieve.

"I really am very tired," Arthur said in a vague attempt at prevarication.

As he expected, it did not work in any way.

"Oh, we are all tired," said the captain dismissively. "And we will all dance, won't we, Mrs. Toussaint?"

"We certainly will, Captain," his wife said, beaming. "And I am sure your wife would greatly enjoy being in your arms—I mean, dancing with you here, eh, Your Grace?"

Heat blossomed in Arthur, more in service of Jojo's shame than his own. For the woman could not have spoken truer. He would greatly enjoy having the woman who was pretending to be his wife back in his arms. He had not forgotten the tantalizing presence when he had first pulled her away from that other dining table, what felt like a thousand miles and a lifetime ago.

But as Arthur glanced at Jojo, he saw only panic and mortification on her face.

His heart skipped a beat. Well, it was foolish to hope she had enjoyed the same encounter. At the time, she had not known if he would use the knife pressed to her side.

It was his contrary nature, he knew, but as Arthur saw just how little Jojo wished to be the center of attention, how desperately she herself wished not to dance, he found himself infuriatingly beginning to wish for the opposite.

"Now, if we move those tables back—," a sailor was saying.

Scraping and banging echoed around the room as the diners

started to rearrange the room for a dance. Arthur tried to use the time to collect his thoughts. They were simple.

Firstly, he did not wish to dance. As a duke, he would be expected to dance something complex, like . . . like La Jolie Flamande. He didn't even know what that looked like! There would certainly be suspicion if a man like him, with the title he claimed, could not dance something like that.

Secondly, Jojo did not wish to dance. The fact was painted clearly on her face.

And thirdly, and most contrary, he wished to dance with Jojo.

Arthur sighed. But there was only one thing he could do, and that was clear.

"My wife and I will retire and allow you all to—"

His words had not finished leaving his mouth before the fiddler, Pierre, began to play.

The tune of a country dance, similar to one Arthur's mother had taught him when he was but a boy filled the room. More cheers went up as people reached for their partners, creating a line of five couples as the music continued.

Arthur's lips parted in a smile. *A country dance. Of course.* Why had he thought this motley crew of sailors would dance anything as complex as La Jolie Flamande? Of course, they would know the sort of dances he had learned as a child.

Arthur breathed in, and boldness filled his lungs as he sensed the change in himself along with the atmosphere in the room. He knew what he was about to do, even if he may regret it later.

Arthur held out his hand.

Jojo stared at it in wonder as though she had never seen a hand before in her life. "Are you sure?"

Not at all, Arthur wanted to say. "Yes."

For a moment, he wasn't sure if she would accept. There was fear in her eyes, hesitation in her expression. He would not have blamed her if she had quietly declined and returned to their cabin. It was what he had suggested, after all, mere minutes ago.

But the soaring melody of the music was doing something

within Arthur, something he could not have expected, and it appeared it was creating the same magic in Jojo.

Shyly, not quite meeting his eye as she nodded, she took his hand.

Arthur almost gasped. The connection—it was more than he had ever experienced. Warmth from her fingers, but more. This was heat, scalding heat, and shivers, and something sparking in him, and warmth pooled in his loins—

"Should—should we get in the line?" Jojo said timidly.

Arthur nodded but still did not move. "Yes. Yes, the line."

They stood for another moment before he shook his head and led her around the table toward the line.

"The duke!"

"The duke and duchess are dancing with us!"

"A full six!"

And the fiddler twirled his bow, grinned a toothy smile, and began.

Arthur had been concerned at first that it had been too long since his mother had taken pains to teach him the steps. Almost twenty years. It was amazing what you could forget from even two years ago. But as the music led him through the steps, he discovered his body knew what to do, even if his mind was unsure what he was going to do next.

Step in, and bow. Jojo curtseyed elegantly and his chest puffed with pride.

She was his.

His dance partner, that was, Arthur corrected himself hastily. It would not do to start thinking of her in that regard. Though it was perhaps too late for that self-reprimand.

As they stepped together and clasped hands, Arthur grinned and Jojo laughed, something in the dance freeing her.

"I believe I then took you riding, isn't that right?"

"Rather forcibly, I seem to remember."

And that was when Arthur lost all consciousness of the dance. He was merely moving, the music moving him, his need to be near Jojo moving him. As she stepped with him up the short line, Arthur had never held his head so high.

Their movements, in time with the music, in time with each other, felt so natural Arthur almost forgot they were surrounded by people. Everyone faded until his senses were filled with nothing but Jojo. Nothing but her beauty, her laugh as she turned on her heels and immediately met his hands once more. Heat flooded through Arthur and there was nothing he could do to stop it.

And he had no wish to. He wanted this dance to go on forever. Everything he had imagined it could be fell by the wayside as the reality of Jojo in his arms overtook him.

It was desire. As the dance slowed and they returned to their original positions, it was desire driving him forward, sparking every touch, increasing his longing with every parting.

He desired Jojo Epwin.

Applause, loud and raucous, broke out around him. Arthur jumped. He had been so lost in Jojo's eyes, in the enjoyment radiating from them, he had hardly noticed they had come to a stop. The dance had finished.

Everything rushed back into focus. Arthur blinked, half astonished to find there was anyone else in the dining hall.

"I had no idea that you could dance like that," Jojo said quietly.

He had expected her to retreat once more into herself, but she held his gaze with a gentle boldness that Arthur had never seen before. He had never seen anything so alluring.

Arthur grinned. "Neither did I."

Other couples were discussing creating a square for the next dance and Arthur grasped the opportunity. Bowing his head and accepting the wild praise he was certain he did not deserve, he took Jojo's hand and led her to the wall.

When he reached it, it was with great disappointment that he released her hand.

They stood for a moment in silence as the fiddler started

playing again, a livelier piece this time, and the four couples began to dance.

Under the noise of the steps and the music, Jojo spoke softly. "I misjudged you."

Arthur blinked. *Misjudged him? How?*

Oh, no. Was it possible that she had guessed? That she had found him out? Was his dancing truly so poor?

"I thought, as a duke—I have met a few dukes, you see," Jojo said quietly, her gaze not on him but on the dancers in the center of the room. "I thought you would be all stiff and stuffy. Standoffish, I suppose. With someone like me."

"Someone like you?"

"Someone without a title, I mean," she replied softly, her lips curving into a nervous smile. "My experience has told me that a title is everything."

How well she understood Society, Arthur thought ruefully. She was right. Half the ladies of the *ton* would fawn over him as a duke but ignore him as Mr. Arthur Hebblethwaite. Why else had he started to pretend he was a duke in the first place?

Not that he was about to reveal his secret, of course.

"I have been pleasantly surprised," Jojo continued. "You surprise me, Fitzpaine."

Arthur swallowed. "Arthur."

"I beg your pardon?"

There was such an intensity in her gaze, Arthur hardly knew how he was standing.

How did she do it? Examine him like that, with no malice nor abhorrence, yet with a piercing view that seemed to peel back the layers of his deceit?

"Arthur," he said again. "It's . . . it's my name."

My real name, Arthur wanted to say. *Not this Fitzpaine nonsense. I made that up! It isn't who I am, and I am tired of being called a name that is not my own.*

Especially by you. I want you to call me by my real name.

"I—but—"

"We are married, after all," Arthur said, with a teasing laugh. "It's probably right that you call me by my first name."

He watched her swallow, watched the delicate curve of her neck.

"I—I think it would be more appropriate, in public, if I called you Fitzpaine."

"Well, I don't care what is appropriate," Arthur said gruffly. "I want you. I want you to call me Arthur, I mean."

Damn, that was almost a slip. And she had caught it, too. Jojo's cheeks were bright red but that only added beauty to her face, rather than subtracting from it.

"Arthur?" she whispered.

It was all he could do not to moan. Dear God, why did hearing his name—his real name—on her lips do such things to him? It was a good thing these breeches were a little loose, or she would soon see the evidence of his regard.

"Arthur," he said firmly.

Jojo nodded. There was something in her expression that told Arthur she rather enjoyed calling him by that intimate name. Maybe as much as he enjoyed hearing it.

"Arthur," she breathed.

Arthur's jaw tightened. *Was this the moment?*

He had never thought there would be one, but after such an evening, it felt churlish to continue lying. He could continue the pretense that had served him well for months, but now it was creating a distance between himself and the woman he—

Not that he was in love, or anything as foolish as that, Arthur reminded himself sternly. No, he was not about to open himself up to a weakness of that sort. He was no idiot.

Besides, how could he admit to the lie now? Jojo trusted him. As she watched the dancers, there was a relaxed air about her that he had rarely seen in her before. She felt safe in his company.

It was the highest honor any lady, let alone Jojo, could pay him. Was Arthur truly willing to lose that now? Her trust meant something more to him than he could explain.

And yet living this lie . . .

"I suppose, being the Duke of Fitzpaine, you have seen many dances like this," Jojo said with a laugh. "Dances far finer."

"Oh, I don't think I have seen anything as fine as this."

She blushed wistfully, true warmth in her eyes. His stomach lurched.

And that decided it. He would not keep on living a lie.

Steeling himself for the conversation that was to come, Arthur drew himself up. "Jojo. I've got to tell you something. I—"

"Ah, there they are, the two love birds!"

Arthur glared but tried to quell it as he saw the captain approach them.

Whether by design or instinct, Jojo stepped closer to Arthur's side, as though for his protection. Pride billowed through him.

"I suppose you two love birds would like to retire to your cabin now to—" Captain Toussaint wiggled his eyebrows, "—sleep."

Arthur did not need to look at Jojo to feel the heat of embarrassment radiating from her. "Yes, thank you."

He had pulled her away before the captain could say any more. The noise of the next dance faded as Arthur closed the door behind them.

Jojo let out a deep breath. "Goodness, I thought—I apologize. You were about to say something."

"I was?"

Arthur swallowed. Looking into Jojo's trusting eyes, it was a painful reminder that revealing his falsehood would teach her not only that he was not to be trusted, but that her faith had been placed in the wrong man. That she had been wrong to trust him. That her instincts had failed her.

Oh, hell.

"Nothing," Arthur said wretchedly. "Come on. Let's return to the—our cabin."

CHAPTER TEN

8 February, 1811

IT WAS A relief to step out onto the deck.

Not that Arthur was making her uncomfortable. *No*, Jojo thought wretchedly. That was the problem. With every passing hour, the Duke of Fitzpaine was getting . . . nicer.

As though he were purposefully attempting to gain her affections.

Which was nonsense, Jojo knew. She was seeing affection there because that was what she wanted to see. She wanted to feel his arms around her again, see him smile, hear his laughter at a jest she made.

Not that she would be bold enough to make one.

Last night had ended suddenly, and quite without any explanation. Why had Arthur—why had Fitzpaine been set against dancing, then changed his mind?

She shivered, despite the warmth of Arthur's coat around her shoulders. The captain's wife had provided her with a pelisse, of course, but this . . . this was a moment when she wanted to feel Arthur's scent around her. It was a shiver thanks to the memory of the dance they had shared, rather than any concern of the weather.

That dance—the way he had touched her! Jojo had never imagined anything so . . . so stimulating. No, that was not the right word. Erotic.

Shame flushed her cheeks as Jojo looked around, expecting someone to be there.

It was most unseemly to even think about such fleshly desires, but she could not help it. Arthur seemed to exude them. Merely to be in his presence was to wonder—

"There you are," came Arthur's voice behind her. "You ate breakfast quickly."

Jojo almost choked on her own words. "I thought—I wanted to—"

"I quite understand," Arthur said, standing by her. "I felt cooped up in there, too."

Her shoulders relaxed as she looked at the dark eyes and sharp jawline of the man who was fast becoming the only person she felt comfortable around. What sort of woman was she, starting to find a duke, and a duke with that sort of glare, comforting?

"It looks like we'll be stopping off at a port soon."

Jojo's gaze flickered to the shore which did, now he said it, appear to be growing closer. "Will it delay our journey?"

Arthur shrugged. The movement was slight, but he was standing close enough to her to brush against her arm. Even through the thick material of his coat, Jojo felt it. She shivered again.

"I don't believe so," he said quietly. "I think it is a planned stop. Victuals and fresh water. That sort of thing. A few passengers are departing, we may pick up a few more."

Jojo's heart flickered. If some passengers were leaving, that would leave a cabin available. Perhaps he was telling her this because he wished to take it and end their arrangement.

She swallowed. It was an unusual one, and not one she thought she could endure much longer either.

Try as she might to keep her eyes open, Jojo fell asleep each night in that large bed highly conscious that merely inches from her was Arthur Hebblethwaite, Duke of Fitzpaine.

A shiver fell down her spine. *Sharing a bed with a man—with a duke!* If the news ever reached the *ton*, her reputation would be ruined. No man would ever look at her. It was scandalous indeed, yet so . . . so natural.

"Did you wish to go?"

Jojo started. "I beg your pardon?"

Arthur pointed to the approaching land. "Ashore. Did you want to go?"

Ah. That made far more sense. "No, I do not think so."

What could there be on shore to distract from the growing attraction she felt for this man who believed she belonged to another?

"Do you think—I wonder if there will be more dancing tonight," Jojo said shyly.

Arthur chuckled. "Goodness, I hope not."

Excitement faded. "Oh."

"I would not like the rest of the guests," he continued in a low voice, "to see the way I look at you when we dance."

Jojo's mouth fell open as she stared into the duke's eyes. *What did he mean by that? Could he possibly—*

"Post!"

Jojo started, stepping an entire foot from Arthur at the sudden burst of sound.

"Post," repeated Captain Toussaint, approaching with a grin. "Oh, dear. I have interrupted a moment, have I not?"

Jojo tried to smile, but it was weak at best.

A moment? Was that what it was called? She hardly knew, her breath caught in her lungs, her mind spinning.

Whatever it was, she hated that it had been interrupted. She only had five or so more days with Arthur. Each day ought to be treasured, and they were slipping through her fingers like sand.

"Yes, we pick up the post at each port," the captain was saying, presumably to a question Arthur had asked. "Most of the time it's only for the crew but would you believe it, there was something today for a passenger!"

Jojo nodded vaguely, hoping the head movement would make him think she was listening.

If only the captain would leave them alone! Every moment with Arthur was precious, every chance conversation with him an opportunity to attempt to untangle precisely what she felt. For, whatever it was, Jojo was discovering to her astonishment that it was only growing.

"Yes, and I thought it doesn't say the Duchess of Fitzpaine, but then the description is quite clear!"

Jojo's attention sharpened. *Description? Duchess of Fitzpaine?*

Her gaze flickered to Arthur who looked just as amazed. Was it possible . . . goodness, surely it was impossible she was not the only one of the two of them who was married?

At least, Jojo thought hurriedly, *she had lied and pretended to be married*. But was there truly a Duchess of Fitzpaine already?

"Yes, blonde curls, a shy expression," Captain Toussaint rattled on. "It's all here!"

Jojo blinked. *Oh, no. Surely not. It couldn't be—*

"Well in that case, are you going to hand it over?" Arthur was saying in a polite yet distant manner.

The captain chuckled. "Forget my own head if it wasn't nailed on! Here you go, and I hope it brings good news. It is a weighty letter, I must say!"

And he held out a large letter, several pages thick.

Jojo's heart was cold. No, it was not possible. Although she had underestimated him before and had been proven quite wrong.

"Thank you," Arthur said firmly, taking the letter as Jojo merely stared, transfixed. "That will be all, Captain."

For a moment, Jojo thought the captain wished to remain, but the dismissal was clear.

Bowing low, he said again, "I hope it brings you good news, Your Grace!"

And then he was gone.

Jojo tried to swallow, but her mouth did not appear to be obeying her. It couldn't be—

"Joanna, an elegant Englishwoman of four and twenty with blonde curls and a shy expression," Arthur read on the front of the letter with a chuckle. "They have you down to a *t*, don't they?"

Jojo's attempted smile was surely unpleasant, but she could do no better.

How dare he! After the agreement they had made, after she had told him most specifically she did not wish to be contacted while in Paris.

"Your husband seems quite eager to find you."

Jojo blinked. "My—my what?"

"Your husband, Jojo," Arthur said in an undertone, gaze flickering along the deck to ensure they were not overheard. "I assume that is who the letter is from? He knew you were taken by the French, I assume he had this circulated to a number of places that you could be."

Her heart was growing colder with every word he said, slowly becoming encased in ice. *Well, Arthur was not completely wrong.*

"What are the chances it would eventually find you," he continued, turning the letter over. "Oh, and a pretty seal, too. A *B*, how strange."

Jojo was doing everything in her power not to panic. Would it be possible to read the dratted thing alone, in her cabin? Would he afford her that privacy?

"Your husband cares a great deal for you, doesn't he?"

She blinked. "My husband? I mean, I suppose so."

Arthur nodded, his interest so blatant it was pouring from his gaze. "I am not surprised. I would be . . . I would care for you a great deal. If I were your husband, I mean."

Jojo's heart skipped a beat.

He was merely being polite, she told herself firmly. This is an awkward situation, and all you are doing is making it worse!

A seagull soared overheard as sailors stomped up the gang-plank, bringing in supplies.

"A very fancy seal it is, too. Your husband must—"

Jojo snatched the letter, unable to bear it any longer. "It's not from—it's from my father."

For a moment, Arthur stared. Then he laughed. "Well, the way you say that, I would guess it is not a particularly warm relationship—but then, what does that matter?"

What does that matter? What does that—did the man have any idea what it was to be a woman in this world? Jojo could almost laugh with despair. Never able to make one's own decisions, never allowed to—

"After all, you are free of him now," Arthur said quietly. "Being married."

Jojo nodded, hardly trusting herself to speak.

Ah. She was married. She was Joanna Epwin. She would have to try to remember that.

"Aren't you going to read it?"

Even knowing full well every line of the letter in her hands would bring her misery, not joy, Jojo could think of no alternative. Besides, Arthur's curious eyes would undoubtedly attempt to overlook her if she read the blasted thing in the cabin. At least here, on the deck, she could step back and devour the bile alone.

Dear Joanna,

Well, you have rudely not condescended to bother writing to me, your own father. I must assume you are still angry at me for the words we shared in our last conversation. I spoke my mind, as you know I always do. I consider you disobedient and reckless, and I will not apologize for it.

I suppose you think I will wish to take back my words. Well, I don't. You are the most ungrateful daughter any man has ever had to suffer, and it has been my constant disappointment that you feel no need to obey me and to carry out your duty.

Do you think I created all this wealth merely to see it dis-

appear in rack and ruin?

I deserve grandchildren. I deserve to see the next generation of Bettencourts, to see the progress of my name continue on. You owe me that, even if they will not bear my name.

Three gentlemen have enquired after you during your absence. I suppose you will say that that proves you right, that by disappearing off to France in a pique—France, of all places!—you have succeeded in sparking their interest.

You always were a troublesome child.

Though I suppose in a way you were correct. A Captain Lister, newly returned from France, in particular has been most interested in you. He is a cad, of course. I would not permit him to lick the mud from your shoes.

But still. My point still stands. There are gentlemen here, Joanna, men who wish to marry you. If I could drum up enough interest in you, perhaps allude to the fact that you are greatly desired, who knows who might throw their hat into the ring.

An earl, perhaps!

You need to be married. But you were always so contrary, never speaking when told, always pretending you had no wish for attention.

Going to Paris was a foolish idea. I wish you had never done it. You cannot avoid the marriage mart forever, my girl, and with each passing month you grow only older, not wiser.

And there have even been the most spectacular rumors! I know you would never be so foolish as to allow yourself to be captured by French soldiers, though I have given instruction that this letter is to be circulated in every French town, if the rumors of your abduction turn out to be true.

Knowing you, I would not be surprised if you had found yourself in some other difficulty, however. We have money, Joanna. Almost anything can be solved by money.

Come home. And that is an order.

I have had a copy of this letter sent to every town, city, and village in France. At great expense, I'll have you know.

Your ever affectionate,

Father

Jojo's breathing tightened as she reached the end of the letter.

Well, she had not expected much better. In a way, it was a relief to have it all out in the open. She had known her father had been disappointed in her, though he had managed until she had left for France to keep that particular sentiment to himself.

It appeared her last-minute decision to forego the London Season and instead take her own money and her own trunk and go off to Paris had removed any hesitation her father might have had in insulting her.

Unfortunately, she was still his daughter. Guilt soared into Jojo's heart as her gaze flickered over some of the more painful lines.

> *You were always so contrary, never speaking when told, always pretending you had no wish for attention.*
>
> *Going to Paris was a foolish idea. I wish you had never done it. You cannot avoid the marriage mart forever, my girl, and with each passing month you grow only older, not wiser.*
>
> *You always were a troublesome child.*

"Jojo?"

The worst of it was, he was right. She was shy and so many people had never seen it, but Jojo could not deny that she was a contrary soul.

She did not want to dress in the finest fabrics and go dancing in Almack's.

She did not want to titter at foolish jests made by idiots merely to stroke their egos.

And as for attending card parties at Lady Romeril's . . . she would rather sit in the servants' hall and polish every bit of silver in the place. Which was saying something. Their townhouse spread across forty rooms.

"What is it?"

Jojo jerked her head up. "What do you—"

"Your face, you've got all pale," said Arthur quietly, concern filling his voice. "I hope—I do hope it is not bad news."

It was on the tip of her tongue to say that with her father, it was always bad news. "It's nothing."

"It's not nothing, Jojo," Arthur said with a wry laugh. "I know the contours of your face. I know when something matters to you."

How did he do that? Say things that felt so intimate, so wildly intoxicating?

Jojo could feel admiration rising and looked back at her letter. The last thing she needed was to make a fool of herself.

Immediately, she wished she had not. Her gaze met the thin scrawling lines of her father's handwriting.

"It's just . . . my father," she said quietly.

"Your father?"

Jojo nodded. "He—he has always had . . . 'high expectations' does not really give justice to the demands."

She should not speak so openly, she knew, but Jojo could not help it. Arthur was looking at her so kindly. There was a part of Arthur, and Jojo was only now realizing just how prominent it was, that was nothing like the stereotypes of a duke. There was true kindness in him, but he hid it well, shoved it underneath the gruffness and the haughtiness.

Arthur grasped her arm. "Demands?"

Jojo nodded. "He always—my father is very . . ."

How could she describe it? The constant etiquette lessons, the way he had berated her whenever she accidently used the wrong fork. The stern glances across Almack's if she dared to not dance every single dance—and of course, each must be with a different gentleman.

Never being good enough. Never being enough.

"I can't explain it," she said helplessly.

Looking at Arthur, Jojo was overcome by a desire to spill the entire truth into his lap. That she wasn't a wife, but an heiress lost in France. That she had disobeyed her father by coming to Paris in the first place, and that he was furious, and when she returned home—

In a sudden movement that made her gasp, the letter was wrenched from Jojo's grasp. And it wasn't a sudden gust, or a curious seagull.

Arthur barely looked at the long letter that was now in his fingers. "Well, we can soon sort that out."

"Arthur!"

But her exclamation did not stop him from ripping the letter in half, and into half again. Arthur did not take his eyes from hers as she did so. Exhilaration rushed through Jojo as he continued to rip the offending letter into shreds.

"Arthur, what are you—Arthur!"

Jojo rushed to the balustrade and looked over it onto the waves as Arthur threw the torn scraps of letter in the air.

White fragments of paper fell from the sky like snow. They fell slowly, fluttering beautifully, twisting in the air then falling onto the waves. The ocean was unhurriedly covered with little scraps of the letter which had caused such distress.

Jojo stared. "Arthur!"

Paper was still fluttering down. He had torn it into so many pieces, the sky still seemed full of it.

She turned in shock to Arthur, half laughing as she said, "Wh-Why did you do that?"

"Because it was making you sad," Arthur said firmly. "And I never want to see you sad, Jojo. Never."

There was such powerful determination in his voice, Jojo hardly knew what to do with herself.

He had torn up her father's letter! It was gone, lost to the breeze and the ocean. She would never be able to read those words of anger and disappointment again.

Then the truth sank in.

She would never be able to read those words of anger and disap-pointment again.

He was a strange sort of duke. But he was a good man. A

better man than she had given him credit for, though he had of course made that slightly difficult upon their first meeting. First meetings that involved knives rarely ended well.

But he must care about her, mustn't he?

"I . . . I . . . thank you," she breathed.

Arthur was looking at her so fiercely, Jojo half thought they were going to kiss again. There was something fizzing in the air between them, something akin to what she had felt when she had launched herself into his arms to prove their affection to the captain.

Oh, if only she had been honest when they had first met. If only she had not lied about being married!

But it was too late now.

"So," said Arthur. "I don't want you to give another thought to that odious man. Instead, think of one who is far better."

Jojo smiled weakly. "I already am."

CHAPTER ELEVEN

9 February, 1811

ARTHUR AWOKE DOING what he had promised himself he would never do.

Reaching out for her.

Pulling back his hand as if he had been scalded, Arthur blinked in the darkness and hoped to goodness Jojo hadn't noticed. The last thing he wanted was to make her uncomfortable.

As though sharing a bed with a man wasn't making her uncomfortable enough.

As his hazy sight grew accustomed to the gloom of the night, something was wrong. Something just out of the corner of his understanding.

He blinked. *Jojo was gone.*

Arthur sat up in bed hurriedly, the bed linens falling from him. He was alone. Not only in the bed—in the room. *Jojo was not there.*

Perhaps if they had been in an inn, he would have panicked. It was certainly not like Jojo to wander off. She was not the sort to pick her way through the darkness. And she had been abducted in Paris, hadn't she, by French soldiers?

But they were not in an inn. The *Liberté* gently swayed as it soared through the waves. There was nowhere Jojo could go that would be dangerous, Arthur was sure.

Which did not explain why his chest was growing tight at her absence.

"Jojo?" he breathed, in case his eyes were deceiving him.

No, he was alone.

Arthur fell back against the head of the bed. He should take advantage of this moment. Perhaps a few days ago, he would have. The entire bed, all to himself? Luxury.

But a creeping, twisting anxiety about Jojo's safety was tying itself around his heart and he could not ignore it. He had to ensure she was safe. Even if it meant leaving the cozy warmth of the bed.

The ship *Liberté* was strange in the darkness of night. Or rather, in the brilliance of the moonlight that shone through the window as Arthur rose and pulled back the curtain.

Moonlight shimmered on the waves beneath him. It was a bright night, not a cloud in the sky. The stars shone, pinpricks of light that glimmered. If Arthur concentrated, he could almost see them reflected on the ever-shifting waves.

It would be light enough for him to wander the corridors, Arthur thought, glancing at his pocket watch. Three o'clock in the morning. What on earth could she be doing out of bed at this time?

His footsteps were soft as he padded along the corridor. The ship appeared quiet. Oh, there was probably a sailor or three still awake, he was sure. Someone to navigate, someone to . . . well, he wasn't entirely certain. What did sailors do on ships, anyway?

But he did not encounter a soul as he slowly stepped up the staircase to the deck.

Arthur's gaze flickered about the wide empty expanse. From this angle, it was easy to forget one was on a ship. It was almost like the theatre, a stage—

There. A heap of woman lying on the deck.

His heart went cold as Arthur's heart skipped a beat. What was she doing, lying on the deck—had she been injured? That was surely the only reason she was lying there, alone in the dark, in the dead of night. *Jojo was hurt!*

"Jojo," Arthur muttered under his breath, racing toward her.

His breath caught in his lungs as he reached her. She was lying on a rug, a blanket lying over her and—

"Oh, hello," said Jojo shyly, looking up, stars reflected in her eyes. "I did not expect to see you. Did I disturb you when I awoke?"

Arthur could barely breathe, his lungs were so tight from his immediate panic at the thought that she had been hurt. *She was just lying here?*

"Disturb me?" he repeated foolishly as his mind attempted to work.

Jojo nodded, smiling shyly. "Yes. When I got up. Did I wake you?"

Truth be told, Arthur had no idea. Probably not. She seemed so perfectly ensconced in the rug and blanket, she must have been here for some time. He had only just awoken.

Maybe he wasn't completely awake. His mind certainly felt asleep still. Arthur brushed sleep from his eyes and tried to think, tried to collect himself sufficiently to speak actual words. In English. That were comprehensible.

"You must be freezing," he said.

Well, he was not wrong. It was February, and the night was bitter. Yet Jojo looked remarkably tucked up and warm. A shiver rushed through Arthur, and try as he might to convince himself it was merely a shiver of cold, he knew the truth. It was a shiver of temptation.

Oh, how tantalizing was that view of Jojo Epwin. There she lay, all alone, nestled in blankets. Why, he could join her. Share her warmth. Perhaps even—

"I couldn't sleep," Jojo said.

Arthur swallowed, and tried to ensure he concentrated on

what was before him—the woman before him. The person he was starting to care about more than himself.

"You couldn't sleep?"

Jojo shook her head. "No, I tossed and turned but couldn't sleep. And so I thought . . . why not come out here?"

She pointed upward, directly perpendicular from the deck. Arthur tilted back his head and looked where she was pointing.

It was spectacular. Arthur had never seen a night so clear nor stars so bright. It was as though the heavens had been opened to them, permission given for that night alone to see more than any other human had ever seen.

"I've always loved stars," said Jojo softly.

Arthur swallowed.

There was such a sweetness to her. Before meeting her, he had always thought—wrongly, as it turned out—he liked his women with fire. Spark. Bold brashness, an argumentative nature, a directness that would reveal precisely what they thought about everything and anything.

Those had always been the women who had caught his eye, anyway.

But Arthur was discovering, much to his surprise, there was something far sweeter in slowly encouraging a shy woman to trust him. To see the change in a woman as she started to realize she was safe with him. To become her confidante, to see a side of her no one else saw.

A part of her just for him.

Arthur's stomach swooped. How long had it been, he wondered dryly, since he had started falling in love with Jojo Epwin? He had barely noticed when it had begun, and it was only now, when he was in too deep, that he realized he had been falling for a while.

Well, there was nothing for it.

"Arthur!" said Jojo in astonishment.

Arthur grinned as he dropped to his knees, pulling at her blanket. "Go on, budge up."

"But—"

"There's hardly room for me under the rug," he pointed out happily, highly conscious of the pink dots appearing in her cheeks. "It is February, you know. I don't know how you expect me to lie down here with you and not freeze to death if you don't move over."

"But I—I didn't think you would want—"

"I want to be near you," Arthur said quietly.

Jojo immediately halted speaking. She swallowed. "You—you do?"

He did. Arthur hardly knew what to do with himself when he was not with her. It was fortunate indeed they were on a ship, for his constant presence by her side was not commented upon, either by her or the crew. After all, where else would he go?

But the idea of returning to their cabin without her . . . no, it was not an option.

Wordlessly, Jojo shifted to the right to permit him room. Arthur tried not to think about just how intimate this was as he slipped into the gap, already warmed by her presence.

Oh dear God.

"You could be much warmer in bed, you know," Jojo whispered, looking not at him but instead at the stars.

Arthur chuckled softly. "What, without you?"

He had already been gazing at her when he spoke. In truth, he was not sure how to drag his eyes away. Those perfect blonde curls, that curve of her neck, the whorl of her ear.

Jojo turned to face him, and as their eyes met, something shifted.

Whether it was within him, or the ship itself, Arthur did not know. He did know the warmth in her look was something new, something unexpected. Jojo had never looked at him like that. As though everything within her was reaching out to him. As though they were finally seeing each other properly for the first time.

Arthur broke the connection to look at the sky.

Because that wasn't true, was it? It was a painful thought, but not one he could ignore. She did not see him. She saw the Duke of Fitzpaine. She saw a man she thought was noble.

How wrong she was.

"The stars are bright," he said foolishly.

What was he thinking? The stars are bright? Was that the best thing he could say?

If only he were not so conscious of how close they were. The slow and steady movement of the blanket above them, their breathing in time with each other. His hand resting by his side. Was hers doing the same? If he shifted his hand, would he—

"I had thought the constellations may look a little different from France," came Jojo's soft voice. "Being so much farther south, I mean."

Arthur nodded, though it was possible she did not notice.

Oh, hell's bells. He was about to walk into another trap, wasn't he? What did he know about constellations? What did he know about geography or the movements of the planets?

"But there's Orion, just as he normally is."

Arthur grunted. *What was he supposed to say?* Ah yes, Orion. That constellation, or star, or whatever it was, that I know so much about.

It was not as though he had ever received an education. Not a real one anyway. The charity school in his village only taught boys from the age of six to eleven, and even then his father had pulled him out to help on the farm a year early. By the time he had turned fifteen and entered—albeit briefly—the employ of the Duke of Wincham, there was nothing Arthur could not tell you about cows, spigots, or scythes.

But stars?

"And there's the North Star," Jojo was saying. "The first star I was taught to find."

Arthur's stomach lurched. "By your father, I suppose."

Tempting as it had been to read the offending letter which had so greatly injured the woman lying beside him, he had managed not to. Ripping it up was an instinct he had followed before he had really known what to do with it.

It had been a relief to hear Jojo laugh. It had warmed his soul as nothing else had.

"No, my mother," came the gentle reply.

Now that was surprising. "Your mother? You have never mentioned her."

Jojo sighed, still gazing at the stars. "I never knew her, not really. She died when I was eight."

She spoke in such a calm, matter of fact way, Arthur was certain it was from practice. Here was a woman, he was starting to realize, who had been alone, truly alone, for a long time.

"You miss her."

"Every day that goes by," Jojo said briskly. "But it's . . . well, too painful. I try to push her from my mind, try to forget, to not think of what could have been."

Arthur swallowed. Perhaps they were not so different after all. "I was eleven when I lost my mother. It is not something one ever moves past, is it?"

It was uncomfortable, being this open, this vulnerable—at least, that was what he had expected. But as he spoke, Arthur discovered saying this to Jojo, in the darkness, in the privacy of the deck on a ship where almost every other soul was asleep—it did not hurt.

"I don't think so," said Jojo quietly. "And yet I have hope."

"Hope?"

"That I will one day find someone who can love me as she loved me," came her gentle reply. "Perhaps in a deeper way. Love me for who I am. Who I have become."

And Arthur gasped.

He had not meant to do it. But then, he had not meant to brush his fingers against hers under the blankets—an unexpected movement—but he had done. The spark of attraction lingered in his palm as he instinctively jerked his hand away. But he could not help it. The pooling desire in his loins demanded more.

Holding his breath, knowing what he was doing was absolutely outrageous, Arthur moved his hand back to where it had been—and found Jojo's hand moving to meet his.

For a moment, time stopped.

Then their fingers intertwined. Arthur could hardly breathe, his heart pounding, as the moment of intimacy lengthened and deepened. Here, alone, their connection unspoken, the evidence of their intertwined fingers unseen, nothing else mattered.

Nothing but them.

"You know," Jojo said softly, turning to face him.

Arthur swallowed as he mirrored her. Her breath was warm, blossoming out into the cold air. It made the deck feel like a mystical place out of time.

This was madness. He was lying on a deck in the middle of winter with a woman who was married!

Yet that did not stop him. Something was different, something changing between them. Arthur knew he would never forgive himself if he did not see where it could lead.

"What?" he murmured.

"When we first met, I thought . . ." Jojo's voice faded as her cheeks pinked.

Arthur squeezed her fingers, hoping she understood the movement as encouragement to continue. He could not wait to hear what she had thought. That he was handsome? That she had never met anyone so dashing? That he—

"I thought you were a brigand."

Arthur's heart skipped a beat most painfully as his body stiffened. "I—I don't . . ."

His voice trailed away as he looked deep into those trusting blue eyes.

Oh, hell. He was a brigand. She had been right. All this time, Jojo Epwin—Joanna, he should call her—had him figured out. Here he had been, thinking he was being clever by weaving this mystery around her, but Jojo didn't need to know he wasn't truly a duke to know he was most definitely a cad.

His heart sank. Just when he thought he had found someone

who truly saw him.

"But that was because I did not know you."

Arthur blinked. *Had he really heard her say that?* "I beg your pardon?"

Jojo chuckled. "See, you are more humble than you ever give yourself credit for."

Oh, God, how wrong she was.

Something in him stirred; a desire, one he had never felt, to be the man she so clearly thought he was. To be noble, humble. Perhaps he could be, if he spent his life with her.

Arthur's heart rebelled at the notion.

If she had been unmarried—well, things would have been different. He certainly would not have stayed on his half of the bed, to begin with.

"You are not like any gentleman I have ever met."

Arthur knew precisely why that was. Because he was no gentleman.

"And you are like no lady I have ever met," he said honestly, his voice hoarse. "Truly. Not just because you're beautiful—"

"You can't say that," Jojo said with a flush, turning to look at the stars.

Arthur did not look away. "And why not? Why not tell the truth?"

"B-Because—well, you just can't, that's all!"

He almost laughed at the shyness in her voice. It was tinged with something he had never heard in Jojo's conversation before.

A desire for him to keep going.

Oh, she may not notice it. Even if she did, she may not understand it. But she was enjoying being flattered by him, so that was precisely what he would continue to do.

"Jojo, it does confuse me that you don't realize how beautiful you are."

He almost moaned as Jojo's thumb started to stroke his own. Did she have any idea what she was doing to him? What fires she was stirring up? What she made him want? The kisses he was inches away from stealing?

"I may be conventionally pretty," she said to the sky. "But I am not what men want."

Arthur frowned. What on earth was she talking about? "What do you—"

"Men—gentlemen, especially—want a woman who can tease," she said flatly.

His stomach lurched, then something farther down from his stomach lurched. *She thought she wasn't teasing him? God in his heaven.*

"One who can flirt, laugh, be witty, enjoy the attention of a crowded room," Jojo continued. "I've—I've never been like that. I am shy, and in the *ton* that is the worst sort of thing a woman could be."

Arthur could hear it in her voice. The absolute certainty she was worthless; that no one would ever wish to love her. Oh, how very wrong she was.

"I don't want this journey to end," she said, a little too brightly as she met his gaze. "I had thought a week a devastatingly long time, and now—"

"Now it seems like no time at all," Arthur breathed.

This time they had together, it was perfect. On this ship they were husband and wife: they could eat together, laugh together, even dance together and no one would question it. On this ship they could almost pretend what they had was real. Arthur could almost pretend that the title he had falsified for so long was real. But when they reached the shore, it would all be over.

And waiting on that shore would be . . .

Arthur's smile faltered. "What about your husband?"

He cursed himself silently the moment the words left his lips. The sparkle disappeared from Jojo's eyes and before he could hold on tightly, she had slipped her fingers from his own.

She sat up. "I'm cold."

"I'll retrieve another blanket," Arthur said hastily, desperate for the moment to continue. "Another two, or even three—"

"No, I think I'll go inside," Jojo said, not quite meeting his eye as she rose. "You stay out here though if you want. Look at the stars."

She had stepped away before Arthur had time to even think of a response.

Blowing out heavily, he watched the warmth billow into the night air, and hated himself for speaking of the one person who would come between them. Why on earth had he mentioned her husband? They had been sharing such a wonderful moment.

And he'd had to ruin it.

Still, he was no fool. He had heard the gentle order to stay here rather than follow her to the cabin.

"You stay out here though if you want. Look at the stars."

Arthur hugged his knees as he tried not to shiver. That was probably a good idea, much as he disliked it. If he followed Jojo Epwin into a room with a bed right now, he couldn't be held responsible for his actions.

CHAPTER TWELVE

10 February, 1811

As Jojo slowly opened her eyes, it was to discover with some surprise that she was in the large bed within the cabin.

At least, that was what the ceiling looked like. And she was surrounded by bed linens, not blankets. Why did she think she should be covered in blankets?

Then it all rushed back into her mind.

The deck. The stars. The conversation. The light touch which had become holding hands, fingers entangled. A conversation which had delved deeper than she believed possible.

"Jojo, it does confuse me that you don't realize how beautiful you are."

"I may be conventionally pretty. But I am not what men want."

Jojo swallowed and glanced to her side. The bed was empty.

She had expected to feel relief. It was, after all, highly scandalous they were sharing a bed in the first place. If her father ever—well, she certainly would not want anyone to discover the truth of how she and the Duke of Fitzpaine had traveled back to England.

A slow smile started to spread across her face.

The Duke of Fitzpaine.

Before she had really known him, the title "Duke of Fitzpaine" would have given her the sense of a stuffy, trite old man who talked about grouse and fishing tackle.

But she had told the truth last night. He had struck her as something of a ladies' man, a gentleman who would do anything he could merely to inveigle his way into a woman's bed.

Jojo shifted, pulling herself against her pillow.

And yes, while he had technically succeeded in this case, Arthur—Fitzpaine—was not like that. He was not like any gentleman she had met, in truth. Why, she did not know.

Tiredness tugged at her eyes. She yawned.

Well, all this was a distraction, wasn't it? They were almost halfway through their journey to England, the temperature growing colder with every passing hour. Before long, they would be home. Then she would never see him again.

Jojo blinked back tears. *This was ridiculous! She was not crying over a duke!*

"I thought you'd be tired," came a knowing voice.

Jojo started. She had been so lost in her thoughts, she had barely noticed Arthur had appeared, opening the door almost silently and holding—

"Oh, my," she breathed. "Is that a pot of tea?"

Arthur grinned as he closed the door with one hand while carefully balancing a tray on the other. "I thought you might be tired after your stargazing extravaganza last night."

Jojo giggled, cheeks flushing. Only someone as overly dramatic as Arthur could call lying on the deck of a ship in a blanket an "extravaganza."

"You slept far later than normal, so I thought I'd take it upon myself to retrieve sustenance," continued the duke, stepping around the bed and carefully placing the tray on her lap.

Jojo swallowed, trying her best not to catch his eye. As Arthur leaned over her, he was so close. She could feel his warmth, was certain for a moment his gaze had drifted to her—

She hastily looked down. No, her nightgown carefully hid

anything that a man may wish to peruse.

Arthur may be a duke, but he was also a gentleman. In her experience, the two did not always go together.

"What do you mean, slept later than normal?" Jojo said quietly, reaching out with the back of her hand to feel the warmth of the small teapot on the tray. "Have you been keeping track of my waking?"

"Your sleeping, your waking," said Arthur softly, sitting on the end of the bed and affixing her with a strange look. "Anything you do, Jojo."

A scattering sensation of warmth filled her whole body. She had never before been so . . . well, seen. Noticed. Observed.

She had always felt, when living in London and forced to attend many of the events of the Season, that being looked at was the worst things that could happen. She had avoided it, attempted to fade into the background. Hoped no one would consider her.

And most of the time, it worked. Jojo quickly learned just what a gentleman wished for in a conversation partner, and she knew she was not it. So she simply made herself unavailable.

But Arthur—he saw her, whether she wanted it or not, and he had evidently not grown as tired of her as she would have expected.

Most unaccountable.

"Now, you always have something different for breakfast, so at first I wasn't sure what to bring," Arthur was saying, a nervous look on his face.

The sensation of being examined returned once more. How often had he watched her eat breakfast? Her nervous eyes met Arthur's dark ones.

Yet the expected discomfort did not return. Jojo had thought being watched again, having someone's attention wholly focused on her, would be mortifying. With others, it had been. But with him, it felt perfectly natural. As though he should have been watching her for years, and now that he was by her side, everything was right.

"So I thought, I'll get you a little bit of everything!" Arthur said with a laugh.

Which was precisely, as far as Jojo could see, what he had done.

Toast. But not just toast: toast buttered, toast buttered with honey, toast buttered with marmalade. Eggs. Two poached eggs, what appeared to be spoonfuls of scrambled egg, and a fried egg. Two slices of bacon. Two sausages. Mushrooms absolutely swimming in butter. Potatoes, sliced thin and fried to within what appeared to be an inch of their lives.

"It isn't enough, is it?"

Jojo's lips parted in astonishment. "You think this isn't enough?"

Arthur was looking most strange. It took her a moment to realize the expression on his face was one she had never seen from the duke before. It was . . . nerves.

"It's just, I didn't want you to be hungry, so I—"

"Arthur," Jojo said, flushing at interrupting a duke with his first name. "It's perfect—it's more than enough! You may have to finish it for me."

"Oh, never fear," said Arthur, a nervous smile quirking his lips. "I've got the appetite of a horse. But you, you were out there last night in the dark, in the cold, far longer than I was. You should eat up. I'd hate for you to get sick, I mean. That would not be good."

Jojo swallowed her numerous questions about just how this preening, determined duke had somehow become a man so concerned about her wellbeing, and looked at the food.

Well, it was all hot and doubtless delicious. It would be a shame to waste it. She picked up a piece of toast slathered in honey and brought it to her lips. It *was* delicious: sweet and sticky, precisely what she needed after a cold night.

"I am sorry."

"Why?" she asked through a mouthful of honey.

Arthur shrugged in that nonchalant way a man had when he

was about to say something vitally important and did not wish anyone to know how greatly it mattered to him.

"I do not wish to become . . . overbearing," he said softly. "It's just . . . well, it feels as though—at least, it feels to me as though we have fallen into the pattern of husband and wife rather quickly. Don't you think?"

Suddenly the mouthful of honey toast was sticking her jaw together and Jojo could hardly swallow.

Because he was right. Perhaps that was the strange, unsettling feeling at the back of her mind she had been unable to encircle with words. *Husband and wife.*

It had been a rushed decision on her part—Arthur had not had the chance to decide if it was a clever idea or not. She had kissed him, told Captain Toussaint they were married, and that was that. And though Jojo wished to agree with Arthur, tell him she had never felt more comfortable with a man than with him, was starting to wonder if they could be . . .

But of course, that was impossible. He thought her married. It was safer that way for both of them. Lord knew what she would be tempted by, spending another few nights in this bed with the Duke of Fitzpaine, if he knew she was unattached.

Arthur was looking at her expectantly. Jojo forced herself to swallow, toast scratching her throat.

"I hope . . . I hope you do not think I am purposefully attempting to take advantage."

Arthur grinned. "It's odd, isn't it? To look at us, most people would say I was taking advantage of you."

How she wished he would.

Her shock at the thought which had rushed through her mind brought heat to her cheeks and heat pooling lower, between her legs.

Those were wanton thoughts! The desires of a harlot, surely!

Jojo was no expert, but she knew gentlemen had these . . . these urges, and struggled to contain them at the best of times. At least, that was what her father had darkly hinted.

Ladies, however? Ladies did not think such things. They did not want such things.

Jojo tried to push the thought from her mind. "It will be strange, arriving in England."

If her thoughts had not been elsewhere, perhaps she would not have been unguarded.

Arthur frowned. "Strange?"

"Yes, strange," said Jojo softly. *Well, she had been this open and vulnerable last night. Why not in the cold light of day?* "I mean, not being together. Going our separate ways."

The words seemed to echo strangely in their little cabin. It had become home for them, the last few days. In a way that Jojo had not yet untangled in her mind, it was more home than her bedchamber in her father's house had ever been.

A jolt jerked up her spine.

She had not thought of Camberley Square as home. She had thought of it as her father's house. When had that happened?

Sadness rushed through Jojo as the realization soared through her. *The moment she had felt more comfortable with Arthur than with her father.* A man who had abducted her at knifepoint, dragged her across countryside, and been forced to share a cabin with her as his pretend wife put her more at ease than her own father.

Jojo could feel her breath tightening as amazement overtook her.

Was she a bad daughter? How could this have happened—or was it more testament to Arthur's charm than her loyalty as a daughter?

"You'll have missed England, I suppose."

Jojo nodded. That was what one was supposed to say, wasn't it? That you missed home.

But England had ceased to be home the moment she had started to fall for Arthur, delight rising at the mere fact of being with him. When had that occurred?

As she lifted her gaze, it met his, and she knew she could not lie to him. Not now, in this moment. Not ever again.

"No, I haven't missed it. Not really," Jojo said, feeling certainty grow within her. "I missed the thought of safety when I was kidnapped by those odious French soldiers—"

"Careful, we had better not say that too loudly here on a French ship," Arthur teased.

Jojo frowned as she pronged a mouthful of fried potato. "You know what I mean."

He nodded. "I know what you mean."

A sort of settled calm fell upon the room as Jojo continued to eat. The bacon was delicious, and as for the mushrooms—

"We will have to get accustomed again to English habits," Arthur said with a laugh.

Jojo nodded. Really, she did feel so much better after having a hot breakfast. It was a marvel what good food could do.

"And with that in mind, my lady Duchess—" There was a teasing air of mischief in Arthur's face now, something she was certain had not been there before.

What on earth was he thinking?

"—greatly honored if you would grace me with the condescension to accept my—"

"Arthur!" said Jojo with a shy laugh. *Her cheeks were pinking, she just knew it!* "What on earth do you want?"

Her words hung about the air as she took in his gaze. It was hungry.

And that was because he wanted her breakfast, Jojo tried to remind herself. It was that simple. He may enjoy holding your hand, but that was all. He was not so foolish as to want—

"Will you take a turn about the room with me?"

Jojo giggled as she moved the breakfast tray to the empty side of the bed. "You cannot be in earnest!"

"I have never been more earnest in all my days," said Arthur, with a twinkle.

Truly, there was so much more to this man than met the eye. Jojo shook her head ruefully as he grinned and leaned back, showing off his broad shoulders and rather sharp jaw. Who would have thought beneath the arrogant and rather haughty exterior, there was this sort of playful gentleman underneath?

"We hardly have anywhere to walk," Jojo pointed out. "This cabin is so small—"

"Oh, on the contrary!" Arthur cut across her, rising to his feet. "We can walk about the ship! I've not been down half these corridors. I could do to stretch my legs and I am sure you could too. That is—only if you wish to accompany me."

Jojo ensured she did not meet the man's eye as she nodded.

Really, this was too far. She could sense a change in him; perhaps a desire to impress in a different way, perhaps a need to be admired by her anew. Whatever it was, she was starting to get lost in the conversation completely. Or was it Arthur's dark eyes she was getting lost in?

She glanced at her nightgown. "Although, I am hardly suitably dressed for—"

"I shall await you outside my cabin, my lady Duchess," Arthur said hastily. "But be quick about it. And do you want that last slice of bacon?"

"No, I—Arthur!"

In one fell swoop, Arthur had snatched the remaining bacon from her plate and shoved it in his mouth.

"Don't be too long dressing!" he said in a muffled tone as he opened the door. "We have a whole ship to survey!"

Jojo giggled as the door snapped behind him.

Well, she never would have thought she could enjoy such merriment with a duke!

It did not take her long to dress. She was well accustomed to tying her stays alone now, and the blue silk gown Mrs. Toussaint had loaned her was a perfect fit, if a little long in the skirts. But that hardly mattered.

Jojo only wished there was a looking glass in the room. She had not been gifted the chance to look at her reflection in months now, and her wild blonde curls probably looked an absolute state—but there it was. She would just have to accept that this was how she looked.

It was not as though Arthur seemed to have any difficulty looking at her.

The wanton thought was swiftly pushed aside as Jojo opened the door.

"Oh my . . ." Arthur breathed.

Jojo attempted, unsuccessfully, to pretend she had not heard him. "Shall we?"

Arthur blinked as though her appearance was so dazzling, he was struggling to take it all in. "Shall we what?"

Shyness rushed through Jojo once again. *Would she ever be free of her crippling inhibition?*

"Oh, yes, the walk about the ship!" Arthur said hastily, thrusting out his arm. "My apologies, I just . . . forgot. For a moment."

Jojo could hardly lift her head, she was so embarrassed. Why did he look at her like that? Though she wished he could enjoy what he saw, she knew it was near impossible. Gentlemen simply did not look at her.

Still, it was pleasant to slip her arm into his and meander slowly along the corridor.

"Left or right?" Arthur asked.

Jojo tried not to think. "Right!"

Their walk took them down a corridor of what she assumed were passenger cabins—she could hear snoring from one of them—and what appeared to be the hallway to the kitchen.

"You know, it was one of the cleverest things ever done on this earth, goading the captain into giving us that roast chicken," Arthur said appreciatively as he theatrically breathed in the delicious scent emanating from the kitchen. "I've never tasted better."

"So you think the French way is better than the English?" Jojo said, trying to inject a teasing tone to her voice.

Arthur chuckled. "Dear God, don't tell the *ton*! They'll string me up by my collar points!"

Their laughter went with them along the corridors. Jojo had

never taken a turn about the room with a gentleman before. She had never been met by appointment at Hyde Park, taken a walk along the Serpentine Lake with another, or conversed with anyone after a dance. If she had the misfortune of being forced to dance, of course.

But now she wondered why. *This was so easy!* Conversation flowed between them as easily as the *Liberté* rolled through the waves. Having her arm tucked into his was so comforting, so natural. She could do this all day. Perhaps even every day.

"If you weren't a duke," Jojo said impetuously, emboldened by the natural drift of their conversation, "what do you think you would be?"

Arthur appeared startled as they slowly ascended the steps onto the deck and the wintery ocean breeze tugged at his coattails. "Why?"

Jojo shrugged. It was a habit her father had deplored. In the smallest act of rebellion she could manage, she had proceeded to shrug often when in France.

"I am curious," she said softly, immediately regretting the impertinent question. "It does not matter, you do not have to answer—"

"I would probably," Arthur said dryly, "be a man of all works."

Jojo blinked. It was almost as though he had an answer ready. "Truly?"

He nodded, his gaze drifting out to sea. "Yes. A man of all works."

"And a master of none?"

Arthur grinned. "Something like that."

They reached the balustrade, but Jojo did not grasp it. That would mean letting go of Arthur, and that was something she would only do when absolutely pressed. Indeed, her free hand had slipped onto his arm too, so she was leaning as close into his chest as she could. Into his embrace.

"If I were a man," Jojo said quietly, "I think I would prefer to be a gentleman."

She felt, as well as heard, Arthur's chuckle. "So would most people. Almost every gentleman will tell you there are still hardships to be found, I suppose, but with the resources to face them . . . I suppose that is what your husband would say, as well."

Jojo stiffened. *Why did he have to ruin this moment, this precious morning, with talk of her husband?*

True, Arthur could not possibly know the husband was a complete figment of her imagination. When he had asked for the man's name, she had panicked and said "Tom." That was all she had revealed about the mysterious man she had apparently married.

She swallowed. "I don't want to talk about him. I would rather talk about . . . you."

Jojo looked at the man swiftly becoming everything she wanted in a companion, in a friend, in a lover. And she saw the same intensity looking back. Was that her affection reflected in his eyes? Or was that his own desire for her?

She looked away before she could investigate and blew out a long breath.

You're dancing on thin ice here, Jojo told herself firmly. And if she weren't careful, she was going to fall.

Chapter Thirteen

"A RE YOU SURE you won't stay a little longer with us?" called out Captain Toussaint.

Arthur tried to give a genteel shake of the head that demonstrated he had absolutely no desire to stay a little longer—without being rude.

Hell and heaven and all the saints. How on earth did these dukes do it?

He had always assumed—erroneously, it turned out—that dukes could do what they wanted when they wanted. Though there was some truth in that, there also appeared to be a great many requirements on a man with a title to be whatever it was the people around him wanted him to be.

Take dinner, for example. He and Jojo had arrived on time when the dinner gong had rung. They had eaten gratefully, for their walk about the ship earlier had given him an appetite.

For Jojo, mainly. A hunger for her that the memory of single kiss on the French port could not satisfy. Though Arthur would not own it to a soul.

But he had also hungered for delicious sustenance, and it was the only appetite that was sated at the captain's table.

They had stayed for at least an hour, listening to Pierre playing the fiddle and another one of the sailors singing a haunting song about a mermaid who fell in love with a fisherman.

The evening's entertainment was rather good. Oh, Arthur was certain any real duke would have heard much better. He would have been to the opera, the ballet, the theater. He would probably have a sister who sang exquisitely, a neighbor who could play the harp.

But he, Arthur Hebblethwaite, knew what it was to make one's own entertainment with very little, and he had been impressed. He had applauded with everyone else. That was what was expected. He was a duke. He was supposed to condescend. But he was ready now to be finished with it, ready to be done with the responsibilities and expectations. Ready to be alone with Jojo.

Because every single moment of this evening, Arthur had been conscious not of the food, nor the conversation, nor the music. No, it was Jojo Epwin who took every fiber of his attention. The way she laughed. The delicate way she tilted her head when she wasn't sure what to say next. That faint flush that tinged her cheeks whenever she thought herself too bold.

Arthur's stomach lurched as they stood in the doorway now, wishing the rest of the ship's company farewell. He had been, in truth, altogether too conscious of Jojo.

"No, truly, we are very tired and wish to retire," he said aloud, as people called out that they should remain for just one more song.

Captain Toussaint nudged Arthur hard in the ribs. "Eager to be in bed, eh?"

The man wiggled his eyebrows most outrageously. Arthur knew, without even needing to look around, that Jojo's cheeks would be flushed dark red.

And so they should, the blackguard!

Arthur leaned close to the captain's ear. He kept a fixed smile on his face as he said, "Mention the word 'bed' in my wife's presence again, man, and it will go hard with you."

When he straightened, Captain Toussaint was the one flushing. "Of course, my apologies, Your—"

"Good night," Arthur said curtly, stepping into the corridor where Jojo had fled.

There was no point in raising the conversation with her. She had evidently heard. Red stained her cheeks and her fingers were twisting together before her.

When had he become so possessive of the woman standing before him? When had he started to say "my wife" and sense no dissonance in his heart?

Oh, hell. He had known himself to be in danger only when it was already too late. Now it was all he could do not to spill his affections into the lap of the woman who would not want them. Could not hear them. Had a husband.

"I—I thank you for being stern with the captain," Jojo said softly, as they slowly walked along the corridor back to their cabin.

Arthur stared. Now that was most unlike the Jojo he knew. She would never even have referred to the shameful comment.

"Retiring early was precisely what I wished," she continued with a gentle laugh. "And if I'd had to listen to one more sea shanty, I would have tipped Captain Toussaint into the sea!"

Their mingled laughter rippled along the corridor, Arthur's shoulders relaxing as they reached their cabin. *Where had this Joanna Epwin been when he had first met her?*

Oh, she was still shy. Arthur knew there was no point attempting ever to rid this woman of her shyness. It was as much a part of her as her blonde hair and shining blue eyes. But rather surprisingly, he had no wish to change it. Jojo being Jojo was precisely what she should be.

Arthur leaned against the door as he closed it, watching his "wife" sit heavily in one of the two chairs in their cabin. "Would you really have thrown him overboard?"

A teasing sparkle was dancing in Jojo's eye. "Perhaps."

He snorted with laughter. "You know, I would never want to fight you, woman."

"Good. I hope you never have to."

And suddenly something shifted between them. Something he could not ignore. A shimmering warmth, a sense of happiness, joy, desperate need to be closer—

Arthur had stepped forward before he knew what had come over him. Startled by his own movement and desperately attempting to hide his true intention, he lurched from Jojo and settled into the other chair.

It appeared Jojo had also felt something, or sensed something, for she had risen from her chair the instant he had made for her. She had similarly altered direction within a heartbeat, half sitting, half falling onto the end of the bed.

He swallowed, tasting confusion on his tongue. *What had just occurred?*

"Tell me," Jojo said softly.

Arthur frowned. "About—"

"Yourself," she said with a shy smile. "I feel like I know so much about you and, at the same time, very little."

Which was precisely how he had attempted to keep it, he thought darkly. The less she knew about him—the real him—the better.

He was no fool. Arthur knew the moment the elegant and refined Mrs. Joanna Epwin discovered he was nothing more than a peasant, she would call for the captain and have him thrown in the brig. If he was lucky.

Yet the tension Arthur had always felt when his false dukedom story was prodded was absent. Was it the French wine he had imbibed that evening? Or perhaps Jojo's far more intoxicating presence?

"I think you know everything there is to know," Arthur said, as easily as he could.

He leaned back in his seat. That was it. Show her with his body he was not sitting on the edge of an anxious precipice.

"I suppose that is true," Jojo said slowly, her gaze never leaving him. "But I know about the man Fitzpaine. Tell me about . . . about your childhood. Growing up in a big mansion out in the countryside."

Arthur almost flinched, but he managed to prevent himself.

Mansion in the countryside? Oh, he had grown up near a mansion in the countryside. The Wincham estate was extensive and had never been more tantalizing than when the Hebblethwaite household had been freezing in their own small cottage for lack of firewood.

"There's not much to tell," he said lazily, hoping she would take the hint. "You speak as though you never lived in the countryside."

"I didn't," Jojo said softly. "My father's house is in Camberley Square—well, to be quite honest it's one side of Camberley Square—"

Arthur blinked as she continued, but he could not follow. *A side of Camberley Square?*

He'd been there once. Sent on an errand when he'd worked for a few weeks at that bookbinder's, fetching and carrying. The Square had been absolutely enormous, almost as large as his childhood village. And she had been raised in a quarter of it?

"—never left the city," Jojo was saying when he refocused. "So tell me. A country life. What's it like?"

Arthur swallowed. Well, she evidently wished to know. He already knew enough about Jojo to know her stubbornness would not permit a change in topic. And he could tell the truth, in a way. It did not have to be the complete truth.

"A country life," he repeated. "Well, do not suppose it is all sunshine and rainbows. I can assure you, it's freezing in the winter, and in the summer—"

"I did not request a report on the weather," came Jojo's gentle reproof. Her eyes were fixed on his, a slight smile on her lips. "I asked about you. Your life."

Arthur hesitated. "Few people are ever truly interested in me."

It was a slip of the tongue, but there was no taking the words back. Besides, it was true, for both Arthur Hebblethwaite and the pretend identity he had taken.

Well, in for a penny, in for a pound.

"I had a difficult childhood."

Jojo nodded. Arthur realized, with a sinking feeling, she expected more.

What more was there to say?

He sighed. "I . . . well. Most people would call it a lonely childhood, I think. An only child, a father who thought little of me. A mother, as I said yesterday, who died young."

There was a sharpness in his voice Arthur hated but had never managed to rid himself of whenever he spoke about being a child. All that effort, all that striving, and they had still been as poor as church mice. Poorer.

"It soon became clear to me my father was unable to help me, and so I . . . I struck out on my own," Arthur said slowly.

Yes, that was true. His father had no trade to offer him, nor anything in the way of encouragement either. Becoming a servant in the employ of the Duke of Wincham had been an obvious choice.

Jojo nodded gently. "That must have been frustrating. Knowing you were to be a duke, yet not having the support of your father."

Arthur opened his mouth, hesitated, then closed it again.

Blast. He had almost forgotten he was supposed to be telling the tale as that of a duke.

"Indeed, my father was not a duke," Arthur said, speaking completely truthfully for the first time in a while.

He almost winced as Jojo's look of amazement seemed to fill the room. "You mean to say—"

"I inherited through my mother's family," he said hastily. *Blast, he could have said something there, confessed perhaps—but no, this was not the time.*

Besides, that did happen sometimes, didn't it? He was almost certain he had heard of a duke who had inherited from his maternal uncle. Or something like that.

It certainly did not seem that Jojo was going to argue with

him. "How fascinating—so you were not raised to be a duke."

Arthur tried hard not to laugh. "Not exactly."

"This life must be strange to you," she continued softly. "All this bowing and scraping, the weight of responsibility. Being on your own, not having a father for support. I—well, I know what that is like."

Sympathy roared through him. Arthur wondered once again what on earth had been in that letter he had torn up. Had her husband made it back to England? Had he and Jojo's father joined together for the search party?

"I have made my own way in the world," Arthur found himself saying. "It is harder, that is true. But I think the rewards, once you attain them, are sweeter."

"I suppose it was hard to leave your family behind," Jojo said softly. "When you inherited the title. I can imagine that must have been a shock."

Arthur was really warming to this tale now. Yes, it all worked—and would make some of his rather more uncouth habits easier to explain. He would have to remember all this when he arrived in England.

The thought of leaving Jojo behind filled him with pain so he pushed it away. They were days away from that—at least two. Perhaps three.

"I prefer not to think about the title," he said honestly. "I prefer to be taken as my own man. Judged on what I do and say now rather than my label."

Where these words were coming from, Arthur could not tell. He had not spoken so truthfully since he had assumed the title of "Duke of Fitzpaine" and smiled glitteringly at the world.

How did she do it? Jojo drew this honesty from him, this complete abandon from falsehood.

Perhaps it was her warm gaze. "That is impressive. Most gentlemen of fortune and name prefer to be judged solely on that."

Arthur breathed a laugh. "I suppose I am not like most gentlemen."

That was when he knew. Beyond a shadow of a doubt, he had to confess.

Jojo had been good to him, kind to him. More. But there would always be this nagging doubt if he did not reveal the Duke of Fitzpaine was a fabrication. Did she admire him for his title, despite her fine words? Or did she truly see the man underneath, the man who adored her?

Arthur took a deep breath. *This could go either way.* But he had to know.

"Jojo—"

"I have to confess something," she said swiftly, the words pouring from her.

Arthur blinked. *Wasn't that what he was going to say?*

Only then did he look beyond himself and realize Jojo was once again tying her fingers in knots. There was something on her mind, evidently, and she had to pour it out. The gap between the chair and the bed was small. Arthur reached out and took her questing fingers in his, holding them still.

She gasped and met his gaze.

"Jojo," he said softly. "You can tell me anything. Anything."

Arthur was almost certain she could hear his heartbeat, then—

"I don't have a husband," Jojo said in a rush.

The words individually made sense. Perhaps if the sentence had come out of someone else's mouth, Arthur would have understood them. But as he stared into Jojo's fearful face, he could do nothing but repeat the words silently in his own mind.

"I don't have a husband . . . I don't have a husband . . . I don't have a husband . . ."

"I—I beg your pardon?" Arthur said hesitantly. Her hands were warm in his. They were twisting again, but this time they were attempting to get away. "Did you say—"

"I told you that I did because I—I didn't know what you were going to do to me when we first met," said Jojo, fear in her eyes. "I thought—I didn't know you then as I do now, and—"

"You are not married," said Arthur in a voice of wonder.

She wasn't married?

Jojo slowly shook her head, a nervous smile emerging. "Are you angry with me?"

Angry? Arthur could barely understand the many emotions now rushing through him. *Not married? No husband?*

Jojo Epwin had no husband. There was no man waiting at the Dover docks for her, ready to pull her into his arms. No husband she was beholden to, no Mr. Epwin to demand satisfaction if he ever discovered Arthur had shared the woman's bed night after night.

She was free. There was no husband.

"You . . . you're a widow," Arthur said in amazement.

Jojo swallowed. "I have wanted to tell you for—"

But the details of her confession mattered little. What did he care that she had lied? *She had told the truth now,* Arthur thought as his heart soared. That meant he could finally make the proposition he had wished to make days ago and do so with little guilt.

A shiver of anticipation rushed through him. *Oh, very little guilt indeed.*

"Jojo," Arthur said slowly. "I have a proposition for you."

She stared curiously into his face. "You do? You are not angry?"

Arthur could not imagine being any less angry. He was almost jubilant, his wishes seemingly granted beyond his wildest dreams.

She had no husband!

"I am not angry," Arthur said slowly. "But I will admit, there has been something on my heart I have wished to say that I have not, for fear of giving offense. Fear of your husband."

Was this the right way? The right time? He had never made this particular suggestion before, and if she were offended—

"My husband that doesn't exist?" quipped Jojo with a wry smile.

Blood and warmth were pooling to Arthur's loins, making it increasingly difficult to think, but he had to concentrate. He had to get this right.

"Jojo," he said softly.

She shivered. "Arthur."

Oh hell, he would just have to come out with it. "I would very much like to make love to you," Arthur said, not looking away.

As he had expected, Jojo's face flushed a dark crimson. "You mean—"

"The thought—no, the desire—crossed my mind a long time ago," he confessed, certain he had to get the whole thing out now before she refused him. *If she could only understand.* "Oh, Jojo, you are so beautiful, so elegant—I have desired you—"

"Desired me?" she repeated in wonder.

Arthur dipped his head for a moment, he could hardly bear it. Who had told her she was not beautiful? Someone must have, for her to have such an ill opinion of herself.

"I know many widows in Society take lovers—there are fewer consequences, particularly with those recently bereaved," Arthur said, trying to keep his words calm as desire blossomed. "And I— oh, Jojo, I would give you such pleasure—"

"Arthur!" Jojo pulled her hands away, eyes wide.

His heart sank. Had he been too forward? Perhaps not explained his desires enough?

"I want to give you pleasure," Arthur said slowly, looking directly into Jojo's flushed expression. "One night. A night of passion, and pleasure, and desire—everything you may have dreamed of. Everything I suspect you never received from your husband."

She did not move away, did not dart to the door and call for the captain.

"You desire me too, don't you?" *Oh God, he hoped he had not been mistaken.* "I've seen the way you look at me, Jojo. The way you cling to my touch. You want me."

Jojo said nothing but did not look away.

Spurred on by her quiet listening, Arthur took a deep breath. "One night. A night of decadent lovemaking, with no consequences. That's all I ask."

CHAPTER FOURTEEN

"I WANT TO *give you pleasure. One night. A night of passion, and pleasure, and desire—everything you may have dreamed of. Everything I suspect you never received from your husband. You desire me too, don't you? I've seen the way you look at me, Jojo. The way you cling to my touch. You want me. One night. A night of decadent lovemaking, with no consequences."*

The words poured through Jojo's mind, but she could hardly take them in. Arthur's low timbre gave voice to tangled words that she had never permitted herself to think before.

Pleasure. Passion. Desire. Decadent lovemaking.

Surely he could not even think of saying such words to her!

Arthur, the Duke of Fitzpaine. He wanted to make love to her! It would be scandalous if it weren't so deliciously enticing.

Jojo tried not to feel, only to think, but that was impossible. She ached for him. The need to be close, her enjoyment whenever she was in his embrace, holding his arm, had her fingers entwined in his—the idea that those sensations could be the beginning not the end . . .

She shivered and dropped her gaze to her hands. It was all based on a misunderstanding—that was the worst part. Jojo realized now just how vague she had been.

"I don't have a husband."

The words had spilled out of her before she could stop them, before she could consider just whether or not she was being clear.

And he had responded. Jojo had never known such passion could exist, but it had poured from Arthur's tongue and she had craved to hear more.

She could not lie to herself. Even if ladies were not supposed to long for such things.

She desired Arthur.

"Jojo?" Arthur said softly.

Jojo swallowed. If she were a good person, she would explain precisely what she meant. Not that she had no husband now, but that she never had. She had never been married. The marital bed was something she had never experienced before.

"A night of passion, and pleasure, and desire—everything you may have dreamed of. Everything I suspect you never received from your husband."

She shivered. Precisely what Arthur meant she was not sure, but it was sure to be something wicked and disgraceful. Something she probably should know nothing about.

So why did she wish to lift her head and say he could take her right there, right then? Why did these longings spring up the moment Arthur started to speak of pleasure?

And, Jojo thought wretchedly, *how would she ever live without him on English shores?*

"I do not wish to pressure you, Jojo." There was an odd expression on Arthur's face—one of genuine contrition. "I have spoken too openly—I apologize, I should not have spoken so to a lady."

Jojo opened her mouth, desperate to reassure, but could not think what to say. That she wished to be kissed by him again? That she could not stop her thoughts meandering to that passionate kiss they had shared when attempting to persuade the captain of their marriage?

She closed her mouth.

How could she say that while allowing Arthur to continue under the misapprehension of her lie?

She was no widow. She was Miss Joanna Bettencourt, heiress, who had been hunted on the marriage mart. Miss Joanna Bettencourt, who had shared her first kiss with a duke who thought he understood her and could not be more wrong. Miss Joanna Bettencourt, whose mind was full of the dark words Arthur had once said, when they had known each other so much less.

"Oh, I think you'll find that for most ladies, where there's a duke, there's a way to convince themselves of the morality of their actions."

Jojo swallowed. The misunderstanding they had fallen under would permit her to take the step she knew most ladies could not take. *Was that wrong of her?*

Arthur leaned back slowly in his seat. "I have shocked you."

"No! Well, yes," Jojo admitted with a shy laugh. "I just, no one has ever—"

"No, I can imagine most honorable gentlemen would rather keep their distance rather than pluck you out of a French den and rescue you," Arthur said, raising an eyebrow.

Shame, red hot and scalding, rushed through her.

So, was that it? Did he see this as some sort of repayment for the service he rendered her? Did he believe she owed him something after rescuing her from the French? She had never considered Arthur to be such a man, but if that's what he was saying . . .

"I . . . I am grateful, truly," Jojo said stiffly, holding herself rigid. "And I am sure my father would gladly repay you for—"

"Jojo—Joanna, that was not what I meant!" Arthur said hurriedly, eyes filled with panic. "You think I would attempt to extort from you something that should be given freely?"

The anxiety that had risen was starting to dissipate, but Jojo's lungs were still tight and there was a strange throbbing between her legs.

"Jojo, anything you permitted—a kiss, an embrace, more—I cannot say what an honor it would be," Arthur said slowly, as though trying to explain. "You are so precious—"

Jojo could not help it. She laughed.

When she looked up, Arthur's face had clouded over. "Why do you always do that?"

"Do what?" she said defensively.

The ship rocked, a wave likely cresting against the side of the *Liberté*. It mirrored the cresting swells of strange expectancy swirling in her stomach.

Could she ever have predicted, as they left the dining hall, this conversation?

"You never accept compliments, do you?" said Arthur lightly.

Jojo's heart skipped a beat. "I rarely receive them."

"And that, I struggle to understand."

"Other people would have said they struggle to believe me."

"You would never lie to me, Jojo," Arthur said seriously. "It's . . . well, it's one of the things I so admire about you. There's not a drop of falsehood in your veins."

He could not have said anything better calculated to increase her guilt.

Jojo looked away, no longer able to hold his gaze. If he knew the truth, how she was permitting him to believe something untrue, he certainly would not wish to make love to her.

The trouble was, she had never been in this position before—*tempted*. Temptation had always been something she had read about. Jojo had never actually been faced with a true temptation. Because that was what he was, wasn't he?

Arthur, Duke of Fitzpaine, was enticing. He would know how to make love to a woman. He was evidently experienced. The single kiss they had shared still stung her lips.

"Jojo?"

She met his gaze and knew. She would never tell him.

How could she risk this moment? This one evening where she could experience everything lovemaking seemed to offer with—as Arthur had said—no consequences?

She had confessed. She had told him the truth, Jojo told herself fiercely. That was enough. *Besides, now he knew she had no husband,*

Arthur would know . . .

The thought jolted through her. He knew, right in this moment, that she was available. For matrimony.

Perhaps this was his way of asking her? It was not something she'd heard done, she thought feverishly, but gentlemen were a strange breed. Perhaps this was what her father had tried to warn her of, though he had always been most circumspect on the details.

"Arthur," Jojo breathed.

Excitement rushed through her. She was going to do it. She would allow Arthur to make love to her.

And just as she was about to speak, to confirm she would willingly take him to bed, Arthur rose.

"Please, forget I said anything," he said stiffly.

Disappointment cascaded through Jojo, displacing all joy. "What do you—"

"I should not have put you on the spot, I should not—"

"No, it's not," she said hurriedly, cheeks flushing. *Oh, it was all going wrong!* "I—"

"—completely unfair of you to expect—"

"Arthur, will you just listen?" Jojo said, almost laughing as she watched Arthur pace about the room, avoiding her gaze.

They were made for each other.

The thought scampered through her mind from a place she did not recognize. But it was true. Every time she thought they were starting to understand each other, there was a confusion— but they always unraveled it.

Was that not what true affection—true love—was? Not being perfect for each other the moment you met, Jojo thought as warmth spread through her heart, but learning together. Growing together. Recognizing the mistakes and then moving past them.

"—outrageous of me to think I could just ask—"

"Arthur!" Jojo said, rising from the bed.

Arthur stopped his pacing, his face a picture of guilt. "I'm sorry, what did you say?"

Her heart beat frantically, but Jojo knew this was the right moment to be vulnerable. To be honest. Truly honest.

"I hesitated because I have never been in this situation before," she confessed, stepping forward but not having quite enough bravery to reach him. "I—this is all new to me."

Arthur gave her a lopsided grin. "What, your husband never requested a night of lovemaking?"

Jojo swallowed.

Would he still wish to proceed, when he knew she had never known the touch of a man? Oh, this tangle she had managed to get herself into! Would she ever find the end of it?

Brutal honesty. That was what she needed to give.

Jojo took a deep breath. "I—"

Yet she could speak no more. In a hurried step that came from nowhere, Arthur closed the gap between them and pressed his eager lips upon her own.

Oh, it was heaven. There was no other word for it—gushes of pleasure roared through Jojo as she accepted his kiss, his hands on her waist, his warmth, his arms—

Everything. She wanted everything.

"Jojo," breathed Arthur as he broke the kiss only to trail further kisses down her neck.

Jojo allowed her head to fall back, giving him room to kiss, to touch. Had ever any woman been held like this? Had any other woman felt so gloriously as one with a man?

"Kiss me," she breathed, half scandalized at her boldness.

Arthur lifted his head with a wicked grin. "I am."

"No, here," Jojo said shyly, touching her lips.

He groaned yet obeyed instantly and she reveled in the power she had over him. How she had managed it, she did not know, but it was indulgent.

Everything he was—duke, gentleman, rider, bold fool—was everything she adored. As tingles of pleasure flickered through her body, Jojo knew she would never experience anything like this ever again.

Being made love to by the Duke of Fitzpaine? No man would ever be permitted to touch her again.

"Tell me what you want," Arthur said in a jagged voice, breaking the kiss that had deepened, his tongue teasing her own.

Jojo blinked, hardly able to see, such hedonistic thoughts rushed through her mind.

She could not say that!

As though he had read her mind, Arthur grinned, his fingers teasing from her waist to her breasts, brushing through the soft fabric where her nipples strained against her stays.

"Tell me," he whispered slowly, wicked grin tilting, "and I'll do anything you want."

Jojo swallowed. *Surely not.* "Anything?"

"Anything."

But as she had decided to ruin her reputation, taking a path with a duke from which there was no going back, why not?

Though her shyness would have prevented her from speaking these words, or even owning to such a thought, Jojo found in Arthur's arms she could say anything. Be anything. Do anything. Share everything.

"I . . . I want . . ." Jojo licked her lips.

Arthur groaned, his fingers scrabbling at the buttons of her gown. "Dear God, I've got to get you out of—"

"Arthur!"

But his hands were swifter than her words. Far faster than Jojo could have imagined, he had stripped her of her gown. The fabric fell in folds to the floor, ever shifting as the waves continued to rock the ship.

Perhaps that was why she felt so giddy. Perhaps that was why Jojo's mind was racing, her legs quivering, hardly able to hold her. Perhaps that was why she did not feel so shy. The distraction of the ever-shifting *Liberté* was far more unnerving than the way Arthur was looking at her.

Heat blossomed in Jojo's cheeks. *Well, perhaps it could not entirely distract her.*

For as she stood in her stays and undershift, Arthur was examining her with a look of hunger new in his expression.

"Beautiful," he murmured as he started to remove his coat and cravat.

Jojo nodded. "Y-Yes. You are."

His shirt was gone in a trice. It was all going so quickly, yet not quickly enough. Jojo's heart was pattering swiftly, her stomach twisting, the warmth between her legs growing apace with every passing moment. She wanted to be back in his arms. She wanted—

"Now," said Arthur quietly as he pulled off his boots, leaving himself merely in his breeches. "You were about to tell me what you wanted."

Jojo looked down. *No, she could not say that. It would be most—*

A gentle finger lifted her chin. When she met Arthur's gaze, it was to see a man who loved her.

Oh, he had not said the words. Not precisely. But he did not need to. She could see the affection. There was desire, yes, but it went further than that. Deeper. He loved her.

"I want," Jojo breathed, not looking from Arthur's gaze. "I want you to kiss me."

He moved immediately to oblige, but before his lips met hers Jojo put out a hand.

Arthur looked at the palm splayed against his chest. "I—I don't understand. You said—"

"I know what I said," said Jojo, hardly able to believe she was about to say this. "What I meant to say was that I want you to kiss me—"

"I know, that's why—"

"All . . . all over," she breathed.

For a heart-stopping moment, she was certain Arthur would turn away disgusted. That was what Society had always told her, hadn't it? That ladies who expressed their own desires, who made demands of men, were nothing better than ladies of the night!

And something had changed in Arthur's expression. A darkening, somehow, of his eyes. A look of shock.

Jojo stepped back, stumbling over her discarded gown. *It had been a mistake to think—*

"God, you're perfect," Arthur breathed. "Your wish is my command, my duchess."

Jojo bit her lip. "But—"

"Where there's a duke, there's a way," he said darkly. "Now, let's get these off you."

Arthur's swift fingers, evidently expert at the removal of a lady's clothing—Jojo tried not to think about that—had within moments removed both undershift and the delicate stays. Shyness threatened to overwhelm as Jojo slowly crept onto the bed, lying on her back and looking at Arthur.

She was naked! Nude, and before a gentleman!

This was it. Before he even touched her, she would never regain her reputation again. She had lost it all, forever, with a man who kissed like—

Jojo gasped. Arthur had covered her body with his own, demanding a kiss without another word. A kiss she happily gave. Her fingers clutched the bed linens as Arthur swiftly moved down her body, trailing kisses to her breasts. Her back arched without conscious thought as his lips took in a nipple, his tongue lavishly swirling around it.

"Oh, Arthur," she moaned, unable to help herself.

"Yes, tell me what you want," he murmured, only breaking the connection between his mouth and her body to speak. "Tell me if you're enjoying it."

Enjoying it? Jojo could hardly think of anything she would enjoy more than the heady weight of him on her, nestled between her legs, as his mouth teased one breast and his hand caressed the other.

This was not precisely what she had in mind, of course, when she had asked him to kiss her all over, but then what she had considered was far too outrageous. Jojo was certain no one else had ever even thought of it! It was only her naughty—

"Arthur!" she gasped.

He had moved again, this time even lower. Now his lips were trailing kisses down her quivering stomach, her secret place aching for—

"God, yes!" Jojo cried, fingers tightening on the bed sheets.

How could she help herself? Just when she had been sure she would never experience it, certain Arthur would be horrified at the mere thought, he had done precisely what she had wished.

He was kissing her secret place.

Warm waves of pleasure rippled through her, making Jojo giddy as she felt his tongue teasing into her.

Oh, this was more than she could have ever imagined! This was everything, this was pleasure as she had never known and never would have dreamt!

And a heat was pooling between her legs, then spreading out, and as Arthur lifted a hand to tease one of her nipples between his thumb and forefinger, Jojo lifted her head in astonishment.

"Arthur, what—oh, yes!"

And then it happened. A rush of pleasure, a sensual explosion that tingled across her entire body, ripping her apart then putting her back together as ecstasy overwhelmed her. She could have wept at the intimacy, Arthur's mouth on her secret place and all of him worshipping her as though she were the only woman left in the world.

When she finally came to herself, Jojo was surprised to see Arthur grinning.

"Now that," he said softly, "was wonderful."

She could hardly believe it. "You . . . you enjoyed—"

"Far too much," Arthur said, his fingers moving to the buttons of his breeches. "Do you want to go again?"

Jojo blinked. *Again? Surely he could not mean . . .*

But her body had already responded to the delicious suggestion, quivering for his touch. The thought she could experience such pleasure again—it made her lightheaded.

Arthur stripped off his breeches, dropping them over the side of the bed.

Jojo stared.

Well, it was difficult not to. She'd seen a few of the marbles in pictures, of course. The Greek gods, the Roman pantheon. Nothing had prepared her for . . .

"I've got a preservative," Arthur said in a low voice.

Jojo nodded, unsure precisely what such a thing was as he returned to nestle between her legs. "I . . . this is—"

"I love you, Jojo," Arthur said, his voice ragged.

And she knew precisely what he needed to hear. "I love you, Arthur—oh!"

He had entered her and though she had expected pain, Jojo felt nothing but a stretching, a filling.

And pleasure. How she did not know, but the mere presence of his manhood within her flickered tingles of pleasure through her body once more.

"Arthur," Jojo breathed.

He met her gaze, and she saw his love there, knew it to be true. The conversation could wait. Right now, she wanted him.

"Love me," she begged. "Please, Arthur—"

He needed no additional encouragement. Arthur's lips met hers as he started to rock, slowly at first, in and out of her. With each thrust a rush of pleasure soared through her. Jojo arched her back, her hips rising and falling to meet his own as the pressure built, as the pleasurable rhythm started to overcome her.

"Faster," she moaned, unable to help herself.

Arthur leaned on his elbows, his lips nuzzling her breast as he increased the pace. "You're so beautiful, Jojo, you feel so—"

"Harder," Jojo said, eagerness to repeat the pleasure rushing through her. "Deeper, Arthur, give me everything—oh, yes, yes, yes!"

The eruption of pleasure was once again a shock, but as Jojo lost herself in the pleasure, she saw Arthur's eyes widen.

"Joanna!"

His shuddering thrusts increased in pace, then stopped. His breathing ragged, his face blissful, Arthur slowly withdrew himself from her and fell onto the bed beside her.

Breathless, unable to believe what had happened, Jojo looked shyly through her eyelashes. She moved into his embrace. Arthur swiftly brought his arms around her and held her as they shared the sweet after-moments of their lovemaking.

Jojo smiled, her eyes closing softly as she reveled in the sensation of being held, truly, by a man who loved her. She would never regret this moment. Never.

CHAPTER FIFTEEN

11 February, 1811

ARTHUR GLANCED OVER his shoulder at the woman whose presence had become a constant warmth on the back of his neck. "Ready?"

Jojo flushed. "Of course. They won't be able to guess, after all. Will they?"

Privately, the man wasn't sure.

Oh, Arthur knew the entire ship was convinced he and Jojo were married from the moment they had stepped on the *Liberté*. They would have assumed, wouldn't they? That the two of them had made love at some point?

If Jojo's kiss on the dock had been anything to go by, the crew could be forgiven for thinking they could barely keep their hands of each other.

But that was then. This was now. And now they had.

"Love me. Please, Arthur—"

A wry smile crept across Arthur's face as he recalled their lovemaking the night before as he stood now with Jojo just outside the dining hall.

Could he have imagined such sweetness? Such boldness? Such pleasure to be shared but, more than that, such intimacy?

It was certainly not something he had experienced. He hadn't known he'd been missing it, in those often brief encounters he had shared over the years with unsatisfactory women.

"I love you, Jojo."

"I love you, Arthur—oh!"

"Come on," said Jojo with a nervous laugh. "Or they'll start to wonder something is amiss between us!"

Arthur chuckled. "They couldn't be more wrong."

She slipped her hand into his and he squeezed it, catching her gaze. His stomach turned as she beamed with complete trust, complete adoration. Her affection could not be clearer.

How had he managed it? How could a man born in what could only be charitably described as a hovel capture the attention and affection of a woman like Joanna Epwin?

"Come on," Arthur said with a sigh, placing her hand on his arm and striding forward. "Or I'll give into temptation, take you back to our cabin, and—ah, Captain!"

He felt the shiver of shock that rushed down Jojo's arm as he almost said aloud what he was sure she had been thinking herself. Would it not be far more pleasant, rather than sit in the dining hall with the other passengers and the rest of the crew, to retreat to their cabin? To where they did not have to share polite nothings, small talk, and continued discussion of the weather but something far sweeter?

Still, it was too late now. They had stepped into the dining hall arm in arm and the captain was beaming over at them from his table.

"Ah, our honored guests!" Captain Toussaint boomed. "Come, break your fast with me this morning, you have not done so for an age!"

Arthur managed to prevent his eyes rolling at the man's exaggeration. No wonder dukes started to believe themselves to be the center of the world. He pulled out a chair for Jojo and ensured she was comfortable. If this was how people constantly treated dukes—and he had no evidence to the contrary—it would easily go to a man's head.

"I hope you slept well?" asked the captain genially, pushing a stack of toast toward them.

Arthur caught Jojo's eye and watched the flush he had known would appear suffuse up her neck. *Well, yes, in a manner of speaking . . .*

"Very well," he said loudly. Then he dropped his voice to a tone for only her ears, enjoying the widening eyes of the woman beside him. "I think I can safely say that I have rarely enjoyed my time so well in any bed. Can't you?"

"How fine the weather is this morning," Jojo cut across him, cheeks blazing. "And the wind, too—so fine."

"Oh, we have been fortunate indeed," agreed the captain's wife. "I was saying to dear Toussaint, I told him . . .'"

Arthur allowed the two women's conversation to wash over him and studiously refrained from catching the captain's eye. He was almost certain the old sea dog would wish to wink, and that he would not permit. No one had earned the right to tease him about Jojo. No man would consider it appropriate to do that to a duke. Would they?

He glanced up. Captain Toussaint winked.

Nodding with a bracing look, Arthur looked at his breakfast and tried to follow the conversation swirling around him.

"—but, of course, if the tides are unforgiving, why, it could take an additional three days to get to England."

For the first time in his life, he rather wished the weather would be inclement and keep him from his destination. Just three more days. That would give him five more days in total.

Five days on the *Liberté*. With Jojo.

She caught his eye. The knowing look they shared shot heat through his bones, melting all resolve to stop looking at her.

Why shouldn't he look at her? Her elegant figure, her blonde hair, her teasing eyes—they all attracted him as they had the first moment he had seen her. But now he had seen all of her. And he didn't just mean in the intimacy of the bedchamber, although that was hardly something to endure. It was also her fears, her passions, her interests. The way she could be bold if she felt safe. The shyness that protected her but was also a part of her, a part she no longer had to hide in his presence.

How had he managed to find a woman like Jojo?

Well, Arthur was certain the odds were against it. There could only be one woman like Jojo in the entire world, and he had managed to be seated by her in a French camp in the middle of nowhere. The odds were astronomical!

Yet somehow he had found a way to her. Being a "duke" helped, of course, but it was more than that. Arthur had never been one to believe in fate. It was chance that guided his life. Chance, and a fair few mistakes. But now, as the clamor of the dining hall rose and he watched Jojo nod as she listened to the captain's wife, Arthur had to admit there might be something in this fate balderdash. How else could he account for the way they had met each other?

"Your Grace?"

Arthur blinked. "What?"

The captain looked a little startled that the Duke of Fitzpaine had replied so rudely, but he only lost his verbal stride for a heartbeat. "You have hardly touched your breakfast, Your Grace. Is it not to your liking?"

Goodness, he hadn't—and the bacon looked wonderfully crispy, just as he liked it. His mind, however, had been attending to other things. Other hungers.

"Ah, I see," nodded Captain Toussaint quietly.

Arthur's gaze jerked. "What do you mean, you—"

"It's easy to see a man in love, especially a gentleman in love," the captain said with a laugh. "I have seen a great many of them in my time and hope to see many more. Your wife is a fine creature, Your Grace."

Arthur swallowed the rising temper that had escalated the instant he had thought the captain was about to be impertinent, and he nodded. *What else could he say?*

Jojo was more than a fine creature, but then, they didn't know her. They didn't see her like he did, didn't understand her character. He saw her—saw her, loved her, knew it was only thanks to her shyness she was not ruling the roost at Almack's.

And now she had revealed to him something Arthur could never have guessed. Something wonderful. Something that would change the rest of his life.

"I don't have a husband."

Her words had rung in his mind ever since she had confessed. To think, Arthur had been convinced he had been carrying the weightiest secret! In a way, he still was.

But just at the moment he had been about to confess, when Jojo could have seen him as he was, the man he had been born not the duke he had pretended to become, she had revealed a secret of her own.

She had no husband.

"Eat, man!"

Arthur started. The captain was still watching, a jovial smile splashed across his face. Evidently he thought the lovesick duke an amusement, he thought ruefully. Perhaps he was.

Determined not to capture the man's attention again, Arthur focused on eating for a few minutes. And the bacon was as good as he had suspected. The trouble was, he could not entirely enjoy it because his gaze had drifted once more to his wife.

His stomach's lurch had nothing to do with his food. *Wife?*

Arthur coughed, thumping himself on the chest as though some tea had gone down the wrong way as his mind spun. *Had he just thought of Jojo Epwin as his wife?*

Well, there was no need to put off the inevitable, he supposed as he returned to his breakfast. They had shared last night, he and Jojo, something that only the wedded were supposed to enjoy, and by God, he had enjoyed it. And there had been a moment— Arthur could hardly describe it—when he had looked at Jojo and seen . . . seen the rest of his life.

At least, what he wanted the rest of his life to look like. It wasn't just that she had looked so beautiful in that moment, but that Jojo had looked back at him with joy, pride, and trust.

Well, there was nothing stopping him, Arthur thought with a roll of joy through his heart. He was unmarried; she was widowed. Why could he not propose?

Propose matrimony to Jojo Epwin. Ensure that he did enjoy her company and her presence for the rest of his life. Know that he would never have to be parted from her. Know that their trust could only grow.

Yes, he would offer marriage, he decided. The moment they landed on English soil.

It would be a fitting way to end their adventure together. They would be out of danger, finally, and off French soil or a French ship. Ready to start the rest of their lives together—

"—you do worry our passengers something chronic, Mrs. Toussaint, and there is no need!" the captain's voice broke through his thoughts. "Why, these winds have been most fortuitous—luck I can only ascribe to the fact that we have nobility on the ship!"

He bowed in his seat to Arthur, who remembered a second too late to incline his head graciously.

Of course. He was still a duke. For now.

"Indeed, if I am not mistaken—and I do not believe I am," continued Captain Toussaint, "I expect we will be arriving in England not the day after next, but tomorrow itself!"

His booming voice rang out around the cabin, causing cheers from the other passengers, and looks of relief from the crew. They were obviously eager to gain some respite.

But it was not joy nor relief that rushed through Arthur at the news. It was . . . well, it felt quite similar to panic.

Arriving tomorrow? Here he had been, hoping he and Jojo would have an additional few days on the ship, but now the captain was saying that he would not even have the time he'd believed he had in the first place! And just after making that promise to himself that he would propose matrimony to Jojo the moment they landed on English soil. Why, if the captain was correct, that would be . . .

Tomorrow.

Arthur swallowed, tasting the panic in his mouth, feeling it tighten his lungs.

He needed more time. Time to prepare.

"Is that not wonderful?" Jojo said quietly, taking his hand far more boldly than he would have thought possible. "England!"

Arthur nodded mutely, not trusting his voice.

England. The place where he had been born, and worked hard, and suffered. The place he had left last year to transform himself into the Duke of Fitzpaine—a man with honor, with nobility. One who demanded respect.

No one in England would respect Arthur Hebblethwaite.

The panic that had leaked into his bones was starting to transform into something else. Something dark, something dangerous. *A temptation to just . . . leave.*

Arthur's heart immediately rebelled against the instinct. He couldn't just abandon Jojo! The thought of leaving her at all caused agony to shoot through his heart, a pain he had never experienced before.

But before Arthur proposed, before he offered Jojo his heart and everything he was, she deserved to know precisely who was making that offer. He would have to tell her. He would have to come clean about his falsehood, the fraud of the title he had lived under for months. And then he would know. For certain.

Was Jojo Epwin in love with Arthur, the Duke of Fitzpaine? Or plain old simple Arthur Hebblethwaite?

"Oh, Arthur, we're almost home!" said Jojo. Following what appeared to be an impulse, she leaned and brushed her lips against his in full view of crew and passengers.

Arthur moved in, desperate to prolong the kiss, audience be damned—but Jojo had already leaned back, cheeks blazing, as a few of the crew whistled.

If it had been in his power, he would have had the blackguards strung up from the mainsail by their thumbs, but he wasn't really in a position to complain.

"Aren't you excited, to almost be back to England?" Jojo said, eyes shining and cheeks flushed. "It's been a long time I know, but your friends and relations will be eager to see you!"

Arthur tried to nod. *Friends and relations.* Well, he had no relations living, and his friends had predominately been whomever he had been working with at the time. No lasting friendships made, no acquaintances he could call on for lodgings or support.

Hell. What was he going to do when they landed in England and Jojo expected to be taken to some sort of manor, or mansion? He didn't even have a full pound on him.

"Excited?" Arthur said aloud, stalling for time, hoping his mind would provide him with the perfect answer to give her.

His heart softened as he took in her excitement.

This was ill news for him, but precisely what Jojo had wished for, clearly. She had never been more triumphant, never more settled as she talked to Mrs. Toussaint. She had been desperate to return to England.

She did not wish to spend more time on Liberté, *with him.*

Arthur pushed aside the thought. *Where is your sympathy, man,* he asked himself. The poor woman was widowed, abducted by Frenchmen, dragged halfway across the country by you, and has spent the last week trapped on a ship with almost no one she knows!

It was only logical she would wish to return to England. To a place where everyone spoke her language. Where she felt safe. Surrounded by those she could trust.

Arthur swallowed. *Hell.*

"Where are you going?" Jojo asked swiftly, the moment Arthur rose from the table.

"Out," he said shortly, hardly thinking what he was saying.

The captain laughed. "You'll not find many places to go out on a ship, Your Grace, but—"

"I need fresh air," Arthur said curtly.

The harshness of his voice did the trick. He may not have a title, but he knew precisely the manner in which to live like he had one. The captain was at least twenty years his senior and they were standing on his ship—yet he immediately bowed his head reverentially at the rebuke.

"Of course, Your Grace—the deck will be empty, you will not be disturbed—"

"I'll come with you," said Jojo, rising and placing her napkin on the table.

Arthur had to say something. Though he hated to say it, he could not bear the thought of having her company when his mind was overspilling with panic. He had lied, and now those lies were about to catch up with him.

"No," he said quietly, placing a hand on her arm. "No, I . . . I need to be alone."

Even standing, Jojo was half a head shorter than him. Arthur's heart skipped a beat as she looked up with bright and trusting eyes.

"Alone?" she whispered, slipping her hand into his own. "Are you sure?"

No, I'm not, Arthur wanted to cry. I'm terrified that I am going to lose you the moment I tell you the truth. I don't know why I did not come clean at the beginning! The minute we escaped from those Frenchmen I should have told you, and now it's too late. Isn't it?

"I'm sure," he said aloud.

A flicker of hurt tinged Jojo's eyes as she nodded and silently returned to her chair.

Arthur felt physically sick. He had hurt Jojo, and that was only by refusing her company for a walk on the deck. For a woman so honest, so open, so vulnerable after sharing such intimacies, how would she react to his constant scheming and lies?

He had to think clearly, and thinking clearly in Jojo's presence was an impossible task.

The sea breeze was harsh against his skin as Arthur stepped out onto the deck. Pulling his coat tightly around him, he tried to take deep, calming drafts of the stuff but it merely scraped his insides, making him cough. The balustrade, thankfully, was cold and solid under his hands. Arthur looked out into the waves, his gaze watching them undulate up and down, up and down.

Well, this was it. He had less than a day to decide precisely how he was going to untangle himself from this mess, if that were possible at all. A day to concoct the perfect speech that would allow him to tell Jojo the truth and for her to forgive him. A speech that would reveal his duplicity, show her he was a good, honorable man who was worthy of her, and convince her to marry him.

Arthur hung his head, his stomach threatening to return his breakfast. How in God's name had he managed to get into such a fix?

And how would he ever find a way to escape it?

CHAPTER SIXTEEN

12 February, 1811

BEFORE THIS MOMENT, Jojo had never known what relief tasted like.

Oh, she had thought she had known. Felt the warmth settling in her stomach, the discomfort in her shoulders melting.

But this was far more visceral than that. This was true relief, knowledge that everything she had endured was over.

"There it is," Jojo said, the relief tasting sweet like strawberries in her mouth. "England. Home."

Arthur's arm was around her. His fingers tightened for a moment around her shoulder.

Home.

For a moment, Jojo hardly knew where to look. At the docks coming closer into view, the shouts and cries from the land easily comprehensible, now they were spoken in English? Or at the man by her side, who had become more like home with each passing day? The man who had brought her out of herself, yet loved what he had found without needing her to be any different? The man who would soon . . .

Jojo pushed aside the thought. *No, she could not expect, she could not presume. Even if she was sure—*

"See anyone you know?" asked Arthur quietly.

Jojo glanced at him before returning her gaze to the shore.

There was something different. The moment the captain had announced they would be arriving early to England, something had clouded Arthur's expression, changing him.

How, she couldn't precisely describe. Perhaps if she had known him longer . . . but no, Jojo was certain no one could know Arthur like she did. Time itself was immaterial. He had opened himself to her as he had to no one else.

And if it had been anyone else, she would have said he did not wish to return to England.

"Jojo?"

Warmth flickered in her heart as Arthur breathed her name. Her nickname, to be sure, the name no one else called her. She liked it that way. It was going to be strange returning to "Joanna" again.

The thought rushed through her mind and she focused, looking for the one person she half hoped, half feared would be on the docks.

Sailors, wearing breeches wider than what was strictly fashionable. Plenty of dockhands carrying goods from one warehouse to another, from warehouse to ship. There were a few people who looked like officials, making notes, receiving reports. Women hawking pies, men hawking ale, a few dogs running about the place. There was even a cat, from what Jojo could see, curled up in the afternoon winter sun.

But the tall man with the harsh brow and glower she knew all too well was not there.

Jojo could not help but feel a little guilt, along with relief.

She should, really, have been wishing her father to be there. It had been months, after all. And he was worried for her safety. Despite only seeing her father's letter for a few minutes, the words were indelibly marked into Jojo's mind.

You need to be married. You were always so contrary, never speaking when told, always pretending you had no wish for attention.

Her resolve stiffened. She may have to return to her father's house for a few weeks, but it would surely not be long before she could leave it for another. One that would be just as majestic, Jojo presumed, but filled with far more love.

"We'll be able to disembark soon," Arthur said softly.

Jojo nodded. "And return to my life."

"Our lives," came his quiet words. "And . . . Jojo?"

She looked up, giving her full attention, heart softening as she saw the fear in his eyes.

Jojo had never met a duke so uncertain of himself. It was definitely not a description she would have used for the Duke of Fitzpaine when she had first met him—but then, she had not really known him yet, had she? Now, with every passing day, Arthur became dearer and clearer. Jojo could see the anxiety pulsing in the nerve on his temple. Feel it in the stiffness of his manner.

What did he have to be nervous of?

"Jojo, before you dash off to this Camberley Square of yours," Arthur said quietly as Jojo's heart skipped a beat, "I would like to talk to you about something. Something important. Once we're on English soil."

Jojo's heart fluttered as heat rushed through her.

"I would like to talk to you about something. Something important. Once we're on English soil."

She had not permitted herself to think about it. *Well, not much.* But Jojo would have had to be blind not to guess what Arthur wished to speak of, once they were no longer on a French deck.

He wished to marry her.

Jojo shivered with the pleasure of anticipation as the *Liberté* rocked as it docked.

Arthur, Duke of Fitzpaine: her husband!

It was a most excellent idea, waiting until they were in England. She supposed there was some sort of rule when it came to dukes. If heirs had to be born on English soil—*where had she heard that?*—it stood to reason that proposals and marriages must follow suit.

She had much to learn, Jojo thought with a rush of excitement. A duchess should know these things.

"Jojo?" Arthur said, gaze serious. "Will you give me five minutes of precious time?"

Jojo nodded shyly. She would give him the rest of her life if he asked for it. When he asked for it.

The idea of spending her years with Arthur, knowing him deeper with each passing month, sharing their lives together, creating greater intimacies than she could have dreamt of . . .

It was about to happen. Jojo could barely contain her excitement as they said farewell to Captain and Mrs. Toussaint.

"I will miss you, Your Grace," said the captain's wife fondly as she curtseyed low. "You may be an Englishwoman, but you're noble. That's plain to see."

Jojo caught Arthur's eye and grinned. How well she had deceived those around her! Why, she had barely thought it possible to trick so many into thinking that she was a duchess!

How had Arthur put it, when he had pointed out her need to practice being a duchess?

"It's easy once you get the hang of it. Anyone could pretend to be a duke or a duchess as long as they had enough confidence."

But for some reason, Arthur did not smile back. He looked morose. Almost hopeless.

It was most unaccountable. Though Jojo attempted to listen to the polite and kind words of Captain Toussaint as he bid them farewell, she could barely take in a syllable.

"—ever need to travel to France, please know my ship is at your disposal—"

There was something about the eyes. Something in Arthur's eyes was deeply despondent. When had this happened? How had she not noticed it before?

"—well, goodbye," the captain finished, gesturing to the gangplank erected for passengers to reach English soil. "Fare ye well, Your Graces."

Warmth suffused through Jojo as she followed Arthur along the gangplank. *Your Grace.* She would have to grow accustomed to that, and as a real title not just as a ruse. She would be his duchess, the Duchess of Fitzpaine.

Jojo shivered as she stepped, finally, back onto England.

England. After so long. After thinking she would die a prisoner, then being abducted by what she had considered to be an evil, scheming man, only now to return as the betrothed of a duke.

Well, almost. Within the next five minutes.

Arthur took a long, deep breath and grabbed her arm. "Jojo."

Jojo did not protest as he pulled her to the side of a warehouse a few yards along the dock from the *Liberté.*

He would not wish to have an audience, she reasoned. Though in a way, she was surprised he wished to propose matrimony the instant they returned to England. Why not wait until he could call upon her at Camberley Square?

Or he could even, and her heart skipped another beat, *propose at his own residence.* Where was the Fitzpaine residence, anyway? She had never heard of it.

"Jojo," Arthur said quietly, standing before her.

Jojo beamed. This man, this wonderful man. He made her so happy. If he would allow it, she would give him the same warmth and happiness and joy. "Arthur. Fitzpaine."

For some reason, he winced. "I . . . I need to tell you something."

She waited patiently. His gaze was darting about as though expecting at any moment—

"Jojo, you know how I feel about you," Arthur said in a rush.

Jojo interlocked her fingers before her and nodded. Perhaps keeping silent would aid the duke in speaking openly.

It appeared to help, although he still would not look at her. Gaze still flickering about them, as though fearful he was going to be noticed by another, he spoke in a low, quiet voice. "I told you how I feel about you and it was the truth, and I am not the sort of man to speak about my feelings—"

"I don't think dukes ever are," Jojo said gently with a shy smile.

She had hoped her words would offer courage, show him she quite understood how challenging this was for him. After all, how often did a duke marry for love? Jojo was almost certain most dukes had their marriages arranged for them, and so Arthur would never have been taught how to do this. Propose, that was.

Perhaps she should make it easier for him.

Though her cheeks tinged pink at the mere thought, Jojo said slowly, "If you have something to tell me—ask me, perhaps—I can already tell you. The answer is yes."

Jojo had thought Arthur would appreciate her efforts. That the tension in his brow and shoulders would immediately disappear and he would pull her into his arms, kiss her, and reveal just how worried he had been at finding the right words to announce his affection.

But somehow, the very opposite occurred. Arthur flushed, his gaze dropping to the ground, and he even took a step back.

A step back from her?

"You are too kind, too good," he mumbled.

Jojo's eyes widened. Was it possible—had she misunderstood? Was the Duke of Fitzpaine *not* going to propose to her?

"I should have asked—told you, rather—a great deal sooner," Arthur said hurriedly. "But there never seemed to be the right time—"

"Arthur? Arthur, is that you?"

Jojo ignored the man's voice behind her. Instead, she reached out and took Arthur's hands in hers. She had to hear what he was about to say.

"Yes? The right time?" she said earnestly. "Arthur, what—"

"I thought it was you!"

And suddenly they were no longer alone.

Well, technically they had not been alone, she supposed. Jojo had been vaguely conscious they were still standing on London docks, teems of people rushing past them. They had never been alone, not really.

But for a few minutes they had felt alone. Jojo could not explain it. Whenever she looked into Arthur's eyes, she could forget the rest of the world and just gaze into his dark expression and know herself to be the center of the world for that man.

But now Jojo saw a rather uncouth looking man—certainly not a gentleman—was clapping Arthur on the back. *And calling him Arthur! The cheek!*

"Arthur," Jojo said quietly, inclining her head to the interloper.

She expected Arthur to push the man aside. She thought the duke would be swift to imperiously order the man away and chastise him for his presumption to boot.

Yet Arthur did not meet her eye. He did not meet the man's eye either. He appeared to wish to disappear into the ground, never to be seen again.

What on earth was going on?

"I haven't seen you for months, you old devil," said the strange man jovially. "What's it been, six months? Seven?"

"And who precisely are you?" Jojo asked, with her best haughty duchess voice.

At least, it was the best she could manage. She had certainly injected it with a sufficiently icy tone to catch the man's attention.

He scowled. "And who the hell are *you?*"

Jojo gasped. *Could he not see, from the quality of her gown, that she was . . .*

As she looked down at her only gown—she had refused Mrs. Toussaint's offer to keep those she had borrowed—Jojo had to admit, she did look rather a state. The gown had seen better days, her hair was unpinned, and there was no pelisse around her shoulders, only Arthur's coat.

Why, she probably looked like a mistress!

Well, thought Jojo, cheeks flaming, *a mistress of a duke still demanded respect!*

"I am Miss Joanna Epwin," Jojo said haughtily, immediately cursing herself for not using "Mrs." as she had done with Arthur. "And you are?"

"None of your business, that's who," the man said insolently.

"Evans," Arthur muttered through gritted teeth. "I'll talk to you later. First I must—"

"I heard you'd gone abroad to seek your fortune," interrupted Mr. Evans, quite rudely in Jojo's opinion. "Though I knew you'd be back. You can't resist the ladies here!"

Jojo swallowed her mortification and tried to remind herself that dukes often were more . . . experienced than the ladies they married. Still. It was rather awful to be so reminded, and by such a brute as this!

"Yes, I knew old Arthur Hebblethwaite would be back," Mr. Evans was saying. "You couldn't make your way in France, though your French lingo was actually quite good for—"

"A duke," Jojo interrupted, putting a little emphasis on the second word.

Well, really! The man had to be shown his proper place. The swiftest way to do that was to remind him of the social difference between the two of them. Really, between the three of them. She had never seen a man wearing such a ragged coat!

But instead of being duly chastised, apologizing, and slipping off into the rabble of the docks as Jojo expected, the man merely laughed.

"Duke? Duke?" repeated Mr. Evans, slapping Arthur once more on the back. "You've not been gallivanting under the falsehood of being a duke, have you, Hebblethwaite?"

Jojo rocked on her feet as though she had been hit by a sudden gust of wind. Her eyes immediately sought Arthur's and, after what felt like an age, pain cascading into her heart, lungs tightening, head spinning, he looked up.

And she saw the truth.

He . . . Arthur, he . . . wasn't a duke?

"You mentioned you might try that old game," continued Mr.

Evans happily, as though he hadn't irrevocably ended all her hopes in one fell swoop. "Trick the nobs you were a nob with them! How long did it last?"

Jojo could barely think, only feel—and it was betrayal cutting through her like a knife.

Arthur was looking at her, eyes now pleading. *Pleading for what? Forgiveness?*

How could she forgive a man for being so outrageously deceitful? For lying—oh God, he wasn't a duke? Who was he then?

Jojo's whole world was shaking, and it was all she could do to remain upright. How could she have been so foolish? Believing a man the instant he told her anything. Falling in love with a man who evidently had never been a part of Society, let alone a member of Almack's. And she had allowed him to—

"—be seeing you at the Old Duke of York," Mr. Evans was saying, utterly oblivious to the agony he was causing. "Look after yourself, you old reprobate, and don't tell any more women you're a duke, you blackguard!" Laughing happily as though it was the best joke ever told, he walked away.

Jojo discovered, much to her chagrin, her cheeks were burning. Heat was pouring through her, shame and rage mingled together that undoubtedly made her look guilty.

Her? She had been nothing but—well, mostly honest.

"So," she said quietly. "Arthur Hebblethwaite. Not the Duke of Fitzpaine."

Arthur winced, though because his falsehood had been revealed or due to the iciness of her tone, Jojo could not tell.

"I can explain—"

"You know, I don't think you can," Jojo said quietly.

How strange. She had thought, if she were ever bereaved again, that she would cry.

Yet as she looked at the man who had utterly betrayed her trust, lied to her, twisted her heart then stamped it underfoot, Jojo found to her surprise that though her heart was breaking, she could tell him precisely how and do so with dry eyes.

Her father, she thought darkly, *would be proud.*

"I never meant it to be like this—I thought I could—I started telling that lie a long time before I met you," Arthur said in a rush.

And she could feel his guilt, but it didn't help her. *How could he have done this to her?*

"Yet you still lied."

"I didn't know how to tell the truth," he said desperately.

Jojo swallowed, almost wishing to laugh, it was all so ridiculous. "I see."

"No, I mean—damn it, Jojo, I'm not good with words!" Arthur said, reaching for her hand. "I'm far better at—"

"Lying," Jojo said softly as she pulled her hand away.

How was it possible to feel this agony, when not a single blade had touched her skin? Jojo's mind spun with the pain, the absolute deathblow of his betrayal.

He wasn't a duke. He wasn't even a gentleman. And she had let him—

"I am sorry, Jojo—"

"Don't call me that," she said, her mouth dry. "You may call me Miss Bettencourt."

The words had slipped from her mouth before she could stop them.

Arthur frowned. "Why on earth would I—as a widow, I presumed you would keep your husband's . . ."

His eyes widened.

Jojo looked away. "This isn't about—"

"You lied to me, too," Arthur said softly. "You weren't ever married, were you?"

That made her look up. "I never said I was—I told you I didn't have a husband!"

"But not that you were never married, and therefore not a widow," Arthur said, frowning in a most outrageous way.

Who was he to lecture her on the merits of truth telling?

Jojo pushed aside the guilt forcing its way into her heart. She had not lied, not really. She had told a lie to protect herself and had attempted to confess the truth. He hadn't let her, that was true—but still, she had tried!

Had Arthur—Mr. Hebblethwaite, as she would have to think of him now—ever even considered revealing his true name to her?

"I . . . I took your virtue."

Heat scalded Jojo's cheeks.

He was inexplicably shaking his head, dropping his voice to a hiss, his cheeks as red as hers felt. "I would never have done that if I had known you were an innocent!"

And her shame, embarrassment, her desperate wish that none of this had ever happened, made Jojo say something even she did not expect. "Well, I never would have let you take it if I had known you were not a duke!"

Jojo clasped her hands over her mouth, horrified at what she had said. But it was too late. The damage was done.

A cold wind rushed by them as they stood in silence, staring at each other. Shouts of men throwing cargo, a seagull squawking in the air. And in this strange mundane part of the world, Jojo knew that whatever trust had been built between them was gone. Forever.

"You only allowed me to make love to you because you thought I was a duke?" Arthur asked quietly, his voice throbbing with anger.

"It wasn't like—I did not mean that," Jojo said hastily. *Oh, how could she explain it? What words could properly describe—*

"That's what you said."

"No, it isn't!" she said, pain in her voice. "It's because—you lied to me, Arthur, let's not forget that—"

"But I was not the social climber here—or at least, not the only one," Arthur said with a dark laugh that shot pain through her. "And here I was, terrified you wouldn't love me if I weren't a duke, and this entire time—"

"It wasn't like that!" Jojo said, her emotions a tangle of bitterness and anger. "Arthur, you were the one who—"

"I don't want to hear it," Arthur said flatly. He took a step back and folded his arms.

And pain, shame, agony at betrayal, and exhaustion overwhelmed Jojo. She felt weary, heavy even, as though the burden of the world had been placed on her shoulders. The one person she thought she could rely on had decided to abandon her.

Abandon them. Abandon what they could have been.

Then out of the corner of her eye she saw it. A carriage, with a crest on the door that mirrored the seal on the letter Arthur had torn up mere days ago.

"Fine," Jojo said softly.

"Fine?"

"Fine," she repeated. Oh, she was so tired. She couldn't fight this anymore, couldn't fight to recover whatever love and affection they had shared if Arthur had no wish to. Finding a way was easier when the person you were finding it with was a duke. But even if he wasn't a duke, you needed a good man.

"Goodbye, Mr. Hebblethwaite," Jojo said stiffly as she turned away and started walking toward her father's carriage.

"Jojo? Joanna!"

But Jojo paid him no heed. The man she had trusted, the man she had loved—it was all a lie. How much of Arthur—Mr. Hebblethwaite—had been true?

As she reached out for the door of the carriage, Jojo knew she was leaving behind all chance of a future with a man she could not trust, and instead choosing what was safe. What was known.

"Ah, Joanna," said her father in a disappointed voice as she settled in the carriage. "You look dreadful."

CHAPTER SEVENTEEN

24 February, 1811

THE NIGHT WAS young, and Arthur knew it was going to end badly.

"I said that was my drink—"

"You son of a—"

Arthur did not even look around as he carefully picked up his tankard before the table it had been resting upon was thrown over.

It was a common occurrence in the Old Duke of York. His reflexes, however, were evidently getting slow, as a little of his beer sloshed over the sides, drenching his fingertips.

"Hell," Arthur muttered listlessly.

Well, what did it matter? Yes, his fingers were now uncomfortably sticky, but that could easily be remedied by wiping them on his breeches. He did so as two harassed-looking serving maids righted his table. He placed his tankard back down as the two miscreants were dragged out of the pub, regulars cheering to see two men so swiftly losing their senses to drink.

Arthur did not cheer. He didn't even smile.

What was the point? All the happiness and joy he had once experienced had been replaced by darkness. It wasn't even an emotion he could name. Just darkness. A numb pain, though that did not make sense.

He had managed, in less than two weeks, to meet the woman of his dreams, seduce her, gain her heart and affections, and lose her, all in one fell swoop. It had to be almost impossible for anyone else to have achieved such misery in such a short length of time.

"I can explain—"

"You know, I don't think you can."

Arthur's stomach lurched at the words they had shared. He needed another drink, though he had discovered in the nearly two weeks since he had watched Jojo—watched Miss Bettencourt walk away, no amount of drink could remove the pain from his heart.

"You only allowed me to make love to you because you thought I was a duke?"

He lifted the tankard. Anything to rid himself of the agony of losing her. Anything to help him forget it had been his foolishness, pride, and arrogance to think she would never find out.

"Look after yourself, you old reprobate, and don't tell any more women you're a duke, you blackguard!"

Arthur sighed heavily as he placed the almost empty tankard down. The pub was starting to quieten now—at least, as much as it ever did in here. With the two arguing men now apparently beating each other to a pulp outside, he could return to his thoughts.

Not that he wished to be alone with them. Or his regrets. Or his shame. Or—

"Is this seat available?"

Arthur blinked blearily. "What?"

That was one of the few benefits of leaving behind his deceit, he thought hazily. He no longer had to concern himself with the precise wording a gentleman would use.

No more "I beg your pardon" or "I'm terribly sorry" or "Goodness gracious me."

No, just plain, honest talking.

"I said, is this seat available?" repeated the man.

He was smiling. Why on earth he had anything to smile about, Arthur could not tell. He appeared to be a gentleman—at least, he spoke with that stilted politeness he'd attempted to mimic, and he was dressed well.

Gentlemen didn't belong here at the Old Duke. This place was notorious for low-level criminality. It was why Arthur had liked it so much the last time he had been living in London.

He shrugged. "Take it."

He had expected the man to do just that—take the chair and move to the table he had presumably come from. But much to Arthur's astonishment, the gentleman, whoever he was, sat and grinned.

"What a place, eh?" he said with a laugh. "My word, yes, I do enjoy a visit to the Old Duke. May I buy you a drink?"

Arthur glared. Whoever this blackguard was, he evidently could not read the room, a vital skill if one was going to last in a place like this. Arthur could not have made it clearer he wished to be alone. He had been sitting hunched over his drink, had not spoken a word to anyone since he had entered—other than ordering the damned drink—and he had given the man a dark glare the moment he had spoken. Which could not explain why the man appeared to be so . . . so . . . cheerful.

Well, there was one way to change that.

"Go away," said Arthur darkly. "Push off."

Rudeness was not unexpected in a place like this, though he doubted the gentleman often heard such insolence. Even more strangely, the gentleman laughed, leaning back in his chair in that nonchalant way Arthur had never quite managed to ape.

It was infuriating.

Bile and bitterness rose. "I jest not, sir. I wish to be left alone. Go and find some other man to—"

"You know, I am quite enjoying this," said the gentleman happily. "Most people would be delighted to drink with a duke."

Ice cold fury rushed through Arthur's chest as his heart stopped for a moment, then remembered how to beat.

Was the blackguard looking for a fight? How dare any man come in here and disturb the snatches of peace Arthur managed to find when he was able to drag his mind away from—

Oh, hell.

"No, I mean—damn it, Jojo, I'm not good with words! I'm far better at—"

"Lying."

Arthur frowned. "Are you mocking me, sir?"

It was a foolish question to ask, he realized at once. Either the man was mocking him and would consider it even more amusing to have riled a stranger, or . . .

"Samuel Dellamore, Duke of Chantmarle, at your service," said the gentleman jovially, inclining his head. "Mocking you? Oh, no, goodness no."

Arthur sighed.

It was just his luck, wasn't it? After all his lies, the women he'd managed to bed, the French captains who had bowed and scraped just to be honored with the presence of "the Duke of Fitzpaine," and now he had to run into an actual duke. If the man was to be believed.

"If you are a duke," Arthur said bitterly, "you'll have the coin to spring for a bottle."

"Of beer?"

"Of something far stronger," he muttered with a heavy sigh.

The Duke of Chantmarle—if he truly was a duke, and Arthur was still not convinced—held his gaze for a moment. It was a rather searching, piercing gaze, and Arthur did not like it.

Then the man nodded. "I see. Of course. I say, sir? Any brandy behind that bar?"

Arthur's eyes widened as old Tom, the barkeep, wordlessly pulled out what appeared to be a bottle from the last century. "Now, hang on, when I said—"

"Excellent—and two glasses, my good man," said the Duke of

Chantmarle easily. "If I am any judge, sir, and I say so advisedly, I would hazard you have a rather interesting story. One worthy of a little brandy."

It was difficult to take in the strange turn the evening had afforded. Arthur watched as a barmaid was sent over with both bottle of brandy and a pair of glasses. She was flushing furiously by the time she reached the table, but for some reason, the Duke of Chantmarle did not seem to notice.

If that was his true name, Arthur thought bitterly. He surely couldn't be the only man about the place lying through his teeth about his background.

"To interesting stories," said the Duke of Chantmarle brightly, filling the two glasses and handing one to Arthur.

Arthur said nothing but took the glass, swigging the entire contents down his throat, and slamming the glass on the table.

It was a miracle steam didn't blow out of his ears. The brandy was potent, far stronger than he had expected.

As Arthur coughed and spluttered, the Duke of Chantmarle said, "I suppose you are wondering why I am here."

"I wouldn't deny that," wheezed Arthur, swallowing hard.

Dear God, what were the French watering their brandy down with? If he'd known the drink was so potent, he never would have—

"I just thought . . . well, the Dulverton Club has become far too dull for my tastes," said the Duke of Chantmarle, as though one easily picked and chose from the very best dining and drinking establishments of London as a matter of course. "And so I thought I'd come here."

Arthur snorted. Trust a duke to look at all the splendor that surrounded him and think "Not enough."

Only a duke could have such arrogance as to come to the Old Duke and presume to sit with the rabble. Only a true duke would have had the confidence to do it. And despite himself, although he would never walk down that deceitful path again, knowing full well there would have to be a different way to find his fortune, Arthur examined him.

Dark eyes. A frame that was elegant yet strong, dressed in a perfectly cut jacket—not too rich, or else he would have stuck out like a sore thumb in a place like this. But rich, certainly. And poor men did not lounge like that.

"Had your fill?"

Arthur started, glaring at the man for being so prescient as to notice what he was doing. "So, you came here to drink with the common man? Escape your troubles?"

He had intended to speak harshly, perhaps even to offend the man into going away.

But it appeared the Duke of Chantmarle could not easily be offended. "Yes, something like that."

Arthur grasped his glass and reached out to pour himself another drink.

What could a man like the Duke of Chantmarle possibly have to worry about? Oh, he had his problems, or what he thought were problems, Arthur thought viciously. The man had probably never gone hungry in his entire life. He had no comprehension of what it was to struggle through life, to not know where you could lay your head that evening, or if the penny in your pocket would be stolen from you by tomorrow.

Common man? Arthur almost laughed. These dukes, they had no idea. No wonder he had been so tempted to slip into their lives and enjoy all the advantages of being "Your Grace."

"Well, us common men have our own problems to deal with," Arthur snapped. "We don't have time to talk to you about yours."

Despite his gruff tone, the Duke of Chantmarle shrugged. "Oh, I don't know."

Arthur stared. *What on earth was he thinking?* "You don't?"

"I think I'd rather have common problems than the one I have now," said the Duke of Chantmarle, pouring himself another brandy. "That's the challenge of being nobility, you see. Well, I suppose you don't. But when you're distinctly uncommon, if you take my meaning and no offense of course, life provides you with rather uncommon problems."

Arthur almost laughed. *This man wanted to him to commiserate, did he?*

"Portrait painted of you didn't get your nose right?" he said scathingly, trying hard not to think about a certain woman whose blonde hair kept shimmering in the privacy of his memories. "Horse didn't win at the Hampstead racecourse?"

Instead of being mortally insulted, which was what Arthur had been aiming for, the Duke of Chantmarle merely chuckled.

"Something like that," he said quietly, refilling Arthur's glass without him needing to ask. "Or then again, maybe something even more uncommon."

Despite himself, for a moment, Arthur was curious. It was tempting to lose himself in someone else's problems, even if they could be swiftly untangled by one of the three things dukes always had an abundance of: money, connections, or a deep glare.

Which did not explain why Arthur opened his mouth and said something completely contrary. "Well, I have a very uncommon problem," he blurted out. "One I doubt someone of your birth has never had to face."

The Duke of Chantmarle's face immediately became more serious. "Indeed?"

"Indeed," said Arthur, goaded by pain, and regret, and the brandy slipping down his throat far more swiftly than was good for him.

"I would be greatly intrigued to hear it," said the duke softly. "If you would be willing to confide in me, naturally."

It was on the tip of Arthur's tongue to tell the man to go to the devil but leave the brandy. How could anyone understand the depths of his betrayal? The depravity which had led him along such a path? The quality of the woman he had lost?

Arthur swallowed as the guilt of his lies and regret of his actions threatened to break his very heart. The pain in his chest was unbearable, like a leaden weight had been placed on his ribcage and was growing slowly larger with every day that went by.

Another day without Jojo.

"Have you ever heard," Arthur said quietly, "of a Miss Bettencourt?"

That would decide it. If this really was the Duke of Chantmarle—and Arthur had been given no reason to believe the contrary—it would never do to ruin Jojo's reputation.

Assuming, he thought with a stabbing pang, *she had not already lost it. Her virtue was gone, after all.*

"Miss Joanna Bettencourt, the heiress?" asked the Duke of Chantmarle nonchalantly.

It was a good thing Arthur had already placed his glass on the table, for he did not have the coin to replace it.

Heiress? He must have misheard the man.

"Yes, Miss Bettencourt is rather a mystery in Society at the moment," the Duke of Chantmarle continued happily. "Her wealth of course has made her an object of great interest, but her manners! So shy, so awkward—"

Arthur forced himself to unclench his fists, which had unconsciously tightened, and resist doing anything rash.

It would not do to break an actual duke's nose.

"—gossip was that she went to the Continent, though why she would do so in a war is anyone's guess," the Duke of Chantmarle said with a laugh. "I hear she's back in Town now, and the vultures have descended."

Arthur blinked. "Vultures?"

The Duke of Chantmarle grinned. "A woman with fifty thousand pounds has to be careful! I would wager almost every man attempting to visit at Camberley Square is nothing more than a fortune hunter."

There was an odd sort of ringing in Arthur's ears which sounded very much like someone had rung a gong far too close to his head.

Fortune hunter? Heiress? Fifty thousand pounds?

And suddenly, it all made sense.

"I was captured in Paris while I was . . . was on my honeymoon."

"I don't have a husband."

Of course. Of course she had lied. What woman wouldn't? Finding herself alone with a strange Englishman after being abducted and ill-treated by the French, what woman—what heiress—wished to be so vulnerable?

And so she had lied, Arthur thought in wonder. She had kept her riches a secret, her innocence a secret, her lack of husband a secret because she had not known him. How could she trust him, a man who had spoken nary a word to her before pressing a knife into her side?

"Sir?"

And when she trusted him, Arthur realized, she had tried to tell him. She had begun with the fact that she had no husband, but his own eagerness for her had forestalled the rest. As comprehension dawned, Arthur could hardly understand why he had not guessed at it.

Jojo Epwin was Joanna Bettencourt, and she was an heiress. And she had loved him.

"Oh, hell," Arthur said weakly.

"There's a story there," said the Duke of Chantmarle with a laugh. "Come on. What harm can it do to tell me? You never know, I might be able to help."

It was unlikely, but Arthur could hardly keep the words in anyway. He had to confide in someone, tell someone the terrible mistake he had made. Then perhaps he could purge it from his soul.

"It all started when I—I cannot believe I am admitting this to you, of all people, but—I went to France and told anyone I met that I was the Duke of Fitzpaine . . ."

It did not take long to complete his story.

The Duke of Chantmarle whistled. "My word. You have got yourself into a pickle."

Arthur nodded glumly. *Pickle wasn't the half of it.*

Oh, it had been a good jest at the beginning. Arthur had been giddy with excitement in Paris, all those people fawning over him, despite the Revolution that had happened years ago. A duke! An English duke! God, he had never eaten so well.

But the seemingly harmless lie had now injured him so greatly, Arthur was not sure he would ever be able to look at himself in the mirror. And as for Jojo . . .

"I wish to goodness I had just told the truth," he said heavily. "Then I might be happy."

"Perhaps," mused the Duke of Chantmarle. "Perhaps not."

Arthur snorted, coming back to reality. "Of course not! You have a great deal to learn, Your Grace, if you're going to spend any time with us common folk. People like us—like me, with the start I had in life, the advantages, or lack thereof—no, people like me, of my class, we don't end up happy. Happy endings are for other people."

His bitterness dripped from every word, but Arthur saw no point in attempting to hide it from the gentleman.

Was it not common knowledge after all? Did not the whole world know that the rich, the nobles, the gentry—they were the ones who shaped their own paths. They chose a way they wanted their lives to go, and it did. Money and prestige and respect, that would get you everywhere. It was for those like him—those who had nothing—to stay nothing.

"Well, I am not so sure about that," the Duke of Chantmarle said slowly.

"What do you mean?"

"I think your problem is rather simple," his companion said unexpectedly.

It was all Arthur could do not to snort again. "Oh, simple, is it? Charming an innocent woman who believed you to be a duke, then her finding out you weren't before you could apologize?"

The Duke of Chantmarle winced. "I did not say it would be easy. But it is simple. As far as I can see, your problem is how you will explain it to the father."

Arthur stared. Perhaps he had drunk too much brandy, for

that made absolutely no sense whatsoever.

"I don't think you quite understand," he said, as kindly as possible.

"No, I think it is you who doesn't understand," said the Duke of Chantmarle with a shrug. "You love her. She clearly loves you—"

Arthur blanched. "You think so?"

Oh, she had said she did. But that had been before. Before she had known him to be such a cad. A liar. A thief of reputation, a despicable—

"You don't need to be a gentleman to hear that tale and spot a woman in love," the Duke of Chantmarle with a dry laugh. "Trust me. And you love her."

Arthur nodded stiffly. Expressing his feelings was not . . . well, men didn't do such a thing. Except with their ladies, he supposed. He had to assume his father had told his mother, at least once, how he cared for her.

Probably.

"So it's the father that's the problem," the Duke of Chantmarle said slowly, as though explaining it to an infant. "Don't you see?"

Arthur did not. "You want me to march up to Camberley Square—me, Arthur Hebblethwaite, a man who's never had more than three pounds in his possession in his entire life. You want me to knock on that door, demand to see the master—if I'm not sent to the kitchens first—and tell him I wish to marry his daughter?"

There was a twinkle in the Duke of Chantmarle's eyes. "Oh, that's about it, yes."

Arthur couldn't help but laugh, brandy sparking dark mirth. "There's no way—"

"Where there's a duke, there's a way," cut in the Duke of Chantmarle. "I'm sending you, it's my idea. Besides, I would say you have more honor and decency in you than most dukes of my acquaintance."

Now *that* Arthur could not believe. "You're pulling my leg."

"You'd be surprised," said the Duke of Chantmarle quietly. "But this isn't about me, or my class, or our foibles. This is about you and a woman who has been hurt, a woman who loves you. Yes, the father will be a difficulty. But isn't an uncomfortable conversation worth the woman you love? Can't you find a way to her?"

CHAPTER EIGHTEEN

27 February, 1811

"Lovely weather," the gentleman said into the awkward silence. The ceramic ringing sound as he placed his teacup back in its saucer was deafening. "For the time of year."

Jojo inclined her head to show her agreement with the dull words. She sipped her tea.

How long had he been here? An hour? Almost two hours?

If she was careful, Jojo could lean very slightly back in her seat and catch a glimpse of the longcase clock standing in the corner of the large drawing room. Her teacup wobbled as she did so, tea overspilling into her saucer.

Her heart sank. *Eleven minutes.*

Eleven minutes? Surely that could not be all. Surely Luke Beauchamp, the Duke of Ashcott, had been here at least three times that!

But as Jojo returned to her position in the armchair and tried not to sigh, she had to admit it was to be expected. Her father's visitors were never entertaining.

"What a pleasant room," the Duke of Ashcott said, waving a hand about the place.

Jojo looked around. She supposed it was. She had never valued the high, wide windows that let in so much sunlight, the soft curtains around them, the chandelier. She'd rarely noticed the Goya paintings. And as for the threadbare rug on the floor, she'd only realized yesterday it was an Axminster.

For years, her father had encouraged her to host parties, and for years Jojo had refused. And for months before she had left for Paris her father had requested—then demanded—that she invite a few select guests to take tea. Again, she had refused. Now she had returned, it appeared her father was no longer waiting for her to send the invitations.

"I must say, I was astonished to receive your invitation," said the Duke of Ashcott in a low voice. "Not that I am offended, of course, but—still. A lady, inviting a gentleman to tea. Most peculiar."

Jojo tried not to show on her face the myriad of emotions rushing through her. It would not do to offend the man. It was not his fault her father was so idiotic.

"It was my father's idea, naturally," Jojo said, as gracefully as she could manage.

She saw with a sinking heart that this simple statement immediately brought distinct relief to the gentleman seated on the sofa opposite her.

"Ah," said the Duke of Ashcott. "Father. Yes. I see."

Did he? It was Jojo's sincere wish that the duke had absolutely no misunderstanding about her desire—or lack thereof—to have tea with him. It was all her father's fault.

"You will have tea with the man, and you will like it!" Mr. Bettencourt had said minutes before the duke had arrived. "He's a duke, Joanna! A duke! Have you ever spent any great deal of time with a duke?"

And Jojo had smiled, or attempted to smile, and forced herself not to think of her ride on the horse with Arthur complaining, the way he had looked at her after she kissed him, their laughter lying on the deck under the stars—

"See, you haven't," said her father promptly, as though he

had through some clever wit and merit outargued her. "I can understand you are nervous—"

"I am not nervous because he is a duke, Papa," Jojo had tried to explain. "It's—"

"I know, all people frighten you," Mr. Bettencourt had said, brushing aside all attempts to defend herself. "But you'll be having tea with the Duke of Ashcott in less than ten minutes, and you will like it!"

Jojo lifted her teacup and took another sip.

In truth, it was not all bad. The Duke of Ashcott did not have much conversation, which was all to the good because she did not want to hear it. She'd had enough of dukes to last her a lifetime.

"You only allowed me to make love to you because you thought I was a duke?"

Forcing herself to swallow the scalding tea, Jojo's eyes watered as she stared at the floral pattern on her saucer. How she had permitted him to speak to her like that—how she had endured it! And yet the agony of walking away . . .

Jojo had assumed it would fade, that once she was returned to her proper home in Camberley Square, all the strain of the past few weeks would melt away. She would realize that this was where she belonged, and she would never look back and regret what could have been.

After all, what could Arthur have given her? A life of debts and deceit? A world in which lying and betrayal were second nature?

"I apologize. I am no great conversationalist, not at the moment."

Jojo blinked. For a moment, she had completely forgotten the man was even there.

"You are not?" she asked politely.

She immediately wished she hadn't. The Duke of Ashcott appeared to be holding back—*surely those were not tears?*

"Have you ever felt the depths of despair?" he said in a low voice. "Have you ever wondered precisely how you could have made such a mistake, one you can never undo that upends your happiness?"

Jojo swallowed. "Did . . . did my father ask you to say that?"

She could not help but ask the question. She would not put it past him. Mr. Bettencourt had happily accepted his daughter's explanation of her adventures and been heartily grateful that she had returned home. And that, it appeared, was to be that.

Still. She would not be surprised if he had asked the Duke of Ashcott to enquire more deeply about her adventures in France. And this would be a rather fascinating way of doing it.

"Your father? No, it is a completely different father that I have wounded," said the Duke of Ashcott with a dry laugh. "The worst kind. A brother!"

Jojo tried to follow this but struggled. A *father that was a brother—so an uncle, then?*

But before she could ask a clarifying question, the Duke of Ashcott leaned back in his chair and shook his head. "I should have married her."

Jojo's eyes widened. *This was simply not the sort of thing that happened to her!* Gentlemen barely talked to her, and when they did, it was typically to ask the location of the whist table or why a certain other young lady had not attended the party.

They did not spill out their hearts about other young ladies!

"Ah," Jojo said helplessly. "I see. Well—"

"It's strange, isn't it, how swiftly one mistake can irrevocably change one's life?" the Duke of Ashcott said, eyes flashing with pain. "When you think you have made the right one, too, it descends one into madness!"

It was a bizarre conversation. But in a way, it was hard not to sympathize. She knew what it was to lose the love of a person you thought you could spend the rest of your life with.

The only difference was that her man had never truly existed.

"—should have proposed, should not have waited," the Duke of Ashcott was saying wretchedly, twisting his teacup around and around in his hands. "When you have love before you, what is the point in waiting?"

Her heart went out to him. There was such tenderness in his voice, such earnestness. Jojo was under no illusion that this was anything other than a true and genuine affection, one which he had somehow lost, it appeared, through a simple mistake.

Nothing like Arthur, she could not help but think. Arthur was the author of his own disaster. He was the one who lied. He was the one who pretended, who tricked her into . . .

But it wasn't quite like that, was it?

Though Jojo hated to admit it, even to herself, she could not help but own that Arthur had not entirely been deceitful. So much of his character had been open to her. His temperament, his interest in the world. Even his past, though of course she now understood better what he'd told her.

"I was eleven when I lost my mother. It is not something one ever moves past, is it?"

"If I could only have married her," sighed the duke. "Oh, that I have lost her!"

Jojo did her best not to frown. Perhaps he and Arthur were simply different, but the longer the man continued to talk, the more the positive attributes appeared to fall on the "Duke of Fitzpaine's" side.

Which was ridiculous, she told herself. She glanced at the Duke of Ashcott, took in his handsome features. He was a real duke.

Yet he was nothing to Arthur. He did not make her heart skip a beat like Arthur did. The Duke of Ashcott was handsome, but he was not attractive. Jojo could not explain it.

True, he may have been unlucky in love as she had been, Jojo thought as the gentleman continued to whitter on about his lost love, *but that did not make him a perfect match.* It did not even make him desirable as an alternative, which is precisely what her father wished, she knew. Why would he invite a duke to tea, unless Mr. Bettencourt wished his daughter to entrap him in matrimony?

The duke sighed. "I do apologize. I am talking about Margaret again, aren't I?"

"Hmmm," said Jojo with a slight nod. "But I do not mind. Please, continue."

Seeing the light in his eyes as the Duke of Ashcott was given permission from a relative stranger to continue talking about the woman he loved, it was clear this was not a passing fancy on the duke's part. He truly loved her. Whoever she was.

Comparing the two men, Jojo knew, was impossible. The Duke of Ashcott was born blue. He had noble blood, noble breeding, and a fortune to boot. Everywhere he went he was welcomed by mamas, though she had heard a few scandalous murmurs about him.

Which was perhaps why this woman he loved had been lost to him. Jojo wasn't really paying attention.

But Arthur? He was not the typical gentleman—certainly not the sort of man her father would approve of. Not wealthy, not noble, with almost no education, and at times no manners.

"And you are like no lady I have ever met. Truly. Not just because you're beautiful—"

"You can't say that."

"And why not? Why not tell the truth?"

A smile slipped across Jojo's face before she could stop it, her stomach swooping. No, Ashcott was nothing to Arthur. Nothing to his wit, or his cleverness. There was far more warmth in Arthur. Far more heart.

"And here I was, terrified you wouldn't love me if I weren't a duke, and this entire time—"

And for the first time in weeks, Jojo allowed herself to consider, just for a moment, the parting words Arthur had said to her in that painful conversation.

He had been afraid—afraid she would not love him if he were not a duke.

At the time Jojo had thought it ridiculous. Did he truly believe her to be that shallow? Was he to malign her character as a parting gift? Could he think she was so . . . so . . .

Jojo looked at her gown. Blue, silk, with gold thread embroidered around the hems and cuffs. She was seated on an elegantly embroidered chair, one that had been in her family for two generations. In her hand was the Royal Bohemian fine china. She was seated by a roaring fire in a room larger, she rather thought, that the entirety of the upper deck of the *Liberté*.

An uncomfortable prickle crept across her chest.

Difficult as it was to accept—and Jojo was certain she would never actually tell anyone she had come to this conclusion—Arthur was right. Perhaps, if he had unburdened himself when they had first escaped the French encampment and told her he was naught but a man, not even a gentleman . . .

She certainly would not have got onto the boat with him. She would not have looked at him in the same way, definitely would not have listened to him. And when he had reached out under the blanket, beneath that starry sky, would she have accepted his caress? Would she have luxuriated in his touch?

Jojo swallowed.

"—hair, so delicately beautiful, I have never seen a woman's like it. Not to say you are not—but there's no point in discussing it. Her brother is against me, and I understand why."

Jojo nodded vaguely. "Yes. Good."

Arthur had been right. She never would have given him the time of day, never would have got to know him. Never would have fallen in love with a man she had thought was a duke.

But what was it she had loved? The title or the man?

"I say, you do look awfully peculiar."

Jojo blinked. The Duke of Ashcott came back into view. He was peering most closely, as though a ladybird had landed on her nose.

"I beg your pardon?" she said, highly conscious of the fact that she had not been listening to the man for a good few minutes.

Heat started to diffuse through her cheeks. *Trust her to offend an actual duke!*

"I said you look most peculiar," repeated the Duke of Ashcott. "Almost as though—I would not wish to cast aspersions, Miss Bettencourt—but as though you were full of regret."

Jojo swallowed a sob just before it managed to escape.

Regret? How would she ever live with the fact she had proven herself to be just as shallow as Arthur had thought she could be? For it was too late now. What could she do about it? How would she even find him again if she wished to make amends?

No, it was hopeless. Jojo slumped in her seat, teacup and saucer precariously limp in her hands. She had lost a man, a good man, who had fallen in love with her without knowing of her fortune, her name, anything. And what had she done?

"Miss Bettencourt," said the Duke of Ashcott, his voice full of concern now. "Are you quite well? Should I call for a—heavens, what was that?"

Jojo's head had snapped in the same direction. It was impossible not to, when such a commotion was occurring downstairs.

Shouting and what sounded like a door slamming. Muffled footsteps and more shouts, a thump as though someone had been pushed against a wall—

But that couldn't be what it was, Jojo told herself sternly. This was Camberley Square. One simply did not have commotions here. Or at least, they never had. It was one of her father's requirements, that everything in his life was calm and sedate and—

"You blackguard!" came her father's voice from along the corridor. "You devil!"

Jojo's heart quickened. *Were they being robbed? Would the duke protect her?*

"What is going on?" asked the duke, rising to his feet and stepping to the door. "What is happening?"

"I don't know," said Jojo, her breathing shallow. "It's . . . it's like it was before."

"Before?" the Duke of Ashcott asked.

She could not reply. It was all happening again, though why

on earth the French would come all this way—but was it not just like this, when her hotel had been stormed by the French in Paris? The shouts, the groans, the thumps, it was all happening—

Jojo screamed as the door burst open, but her voice cut out abruptly as she took in the sight of the panting man who stood in the doorway.

Arthur Hebblethwaite.

"Arthur," Jojo breathed, heart stopping.

All sound faded away and there was nothing but him. Arthur. Tall and dark, eyes desperately searching for her in the room, chest heaving with the effort.

And then his gaze met hers. "Jojo."

"Jojo?" the Duke of Ashcott said behind her. "Who the devil is—"

"Arthur," Jojo repeated, stepping forward.

She had to be with him. Had to be close, feel her hands in his. The moment she saw him, all her fears and concerns faded away. Something shifted in Arthur's expression as he stepped toward her in turn, but before he could reach her—

"Get your hands off me!"

Jojo screamed.

Hands had suddenly appeared from behind Arthur—hands she could now see belonged to Epwin, their butler, and two footmen. They had grabbed Arthur and were pulling him back toward the corridor.

They were taking him away from her.

"No—Arthur—"

"Jojo!" bellowed Arthur, struggling against the three men and somehow managing to slow them down. "Jojo—let me go, you brutes!"

Jojo froze. This could not be happening—yet she had never seen anything more real.

"Release him."

For a moment, she thought the Duke of Ashcott had issued the order. It was certainly complied with almost instantly, the three servants letting go of the struggling man.

It was only after a few more heartbeats that Jojo realized. It was her. She had said it.

"My word," came the Duke of Ashcott's words behind her. "I did not realize you had another appointment."

Jojo almost laughed. It was all so ridiculous! Here were two men, one wholly suitable and apt, by Society's standards worthy of her hand in marriage. And the other . . .

But this wasn't a time for reason, or aptness, or suitability. Not when such joy had risen in her the moment she had seen it was Arthur struggling to reach her.

"I know my father asked you for tea this afternoon," Jojo said, turning from Arthur with great difficulty and looking at the Duke of Ashcott. "And that was because he wants you to marry me."

The Duke of Ashcott's eyes widened. "Now hang on a moment—"

"But I do not wish to marry you," Jojo said quietly.

She had thought he would be relieved, but there was almost a piqued look on his face.

"Why the devil not?"

Ignoring his question, Jojo turned back to the one man in the world she knew she could marry. The one she could be herself with, the nervous and shy parts of her just as much as the flirtatious parts.

"Because," Jojo said softly, "I want to marry him."

Arthur's eyes widened.

Epwin, the butler whose name she had borrowed while in France, went bright red. "You—you can't, Miss—"

"I do," she said simply.

"No, you can't," said Arthur, dropping his voice as he approached. He halted a foot away, as though nervous that if he got too close, he would lose all resolve. "I lied to you, Jojo, and I should never—"

"It doesn't matter what happened in the past," Jojo said fiercely, words pouring from her heart as they never had done. "The past? We both made mistakes there, Arthur, and I don't want to return to that life again. I want to find a way to forgive each other, to move past it—to build something new. Something true."

Being so close without the comfort of his touch was painful, but Jojo forced herself to continue gazing into his eyes. Would he understand?

A lopsided grin teased across Arthur's lips. "I've already forgiven you—though in truth, Jojo, I don't think you needed forgiving. The . . . the question is, h-have you forgiven—"

Words were no longer necessary. The impulse Jojo had been forcing down the moment she had seen him rose up, unbidden and impossible to ignore.

Closing the gap in one swift step, Jojo kissed Arthur hard on the lips.

"My word!" breathed the Duke of Ashcott.

The servants were gasping but that could not be possible, for Jojo was almost certain she and Arthur were alone in the world. His strong hands around her, his teasing lips parting her own to share and partake in their mutual pleasure. The ripples of delight cascading down her body, the way every part of her was on fire, desperate for his touch—

Heavy footsteps suddenly halted in the doorway, and even lost as she was in the kiss, Jojo knew this was a moment she had to face. For the last time.

Breaking off the kiss, Jojo kept her arm around Arthur's waist as she looked over his shoulder. "Ah, Papa."

Arthur hurriedly turned around. "Sir, I wish to—"

"Papa, I have an announcement to make," Jojo said, forcing past her shyness and knowing this was the beginning of something truly wonderful. Something that would last the rest of her life.

Her father's gaze alighted on the man by her side. At the way her arm was around his waist. "Lord . . . ?" he said hopefully.

Jojo grinned. "*Mr.* Arthur Hebblethwaite. Just mister. My mister."

CHAPTER NINETEEN

15 March, 1811

"THIS IS RIDICULOUS," said Arthur sharply. "Where are we—"

"The more you talk, the longer this is going to take," came Jojo's voice from somewhere to his left. "Just do what I say!"

"Like I ever do anything else anymore," Arthur quipped with a grin.

A gentle shove to his arm told him precisely what his betrothed thought of that particular jest. He couldn't have said what her expression was, however. The blindfold was a little challenging in that regard.

"Are you certain this is necessary?" he asked, stumbling over something on the pavement.

Just as he was about to topple over, Arthur felt his arm being taken by soft, warm hands. Hands he knew well. Hands he would rather have under the linen of his shirt and the wool of his coat, rather than over them.

"Necessary?" Jojo paused to consider for a moment. "Yes."

Arthur groaned. Her laughter rang in his ears, making the entire enterprise worthwhile. He would suffer through a great deal, more than a strange wander down a street with a blindfold on, if he could make Jojo Bettencourt laugh.

Though of course, she would not be Bettencourt for very long.

"Where did you get the name Epwin from, anyway?" Arthur asked, taking another step and disliking most heartily how the world seemed to spin when he did so. Never before had he realized just how crucial it was, being able to see.

"Our butler," came Jojo's voice with a teasing laugh. "Are you sure you cannot see?"

"I am in the dark, both literally and figuratively," said Arthur, trying to keep the impatience from his voice. "Jojo, when you said you were going to blindfold me—"

"Yes, I thought there was far too happy a gleam in your eye," breathed Jojo's voice with just a hint of scandalized tones to make it perfectly clear to him, vision or not, what she thought of that idea.

Arthur groaned. She was a tease, this woman, and he was rather delighted in being teased by her, most of the time. He was currently unsure whether this was one of those times.

"Honestly, people passing us by must think we are absolutely mad," muttered Arthur.

Another squeeze on his arm. "Perhaps. But we are almost there."

She had been saying that the moment she had led him out of Camberley Square, and they still did not seem to be any closer to wherever it was she wished to take him.

Why she had to blindfold him, he did not know. Arthur dreaded to think what the people of London walking past them would think. The gossip pages would be full of it—even more full than when their engagement had been announced in the first place.

"This isn't some cruel punishment of your father's, is it?" Arthur said nervously as Jojo guided him around what felt like a corner. "He hasn't spoken two words to me, you know."

"He sits in the same room with you now," came Jojo's voice, speaking as though he was not being completely fair to her father.

Arthur snorted.

That was some concession, which Mr. Bettencourt had made perfectly clear. How precisely the two of them were going to get along . . . well, Arthur was still making enquiries, but he had heard some lovely things about the north. Perhaps a few hundred miles between himself and his father-in-law would ease the discomfort for both of them.

"You have to remember I am all my father has left." Jojo's voice was quiet, almost obscured by the sound of their footsteps, but it was full of complex emotion Arthur could not understand, even if he could have seen her. "And he has not forbidden the marriage, has he?"

Arthur snorted. "Not with his words, no."

"Arthur!"

"Well, I am doing my best, I am sure," he said, trying to inject more buoyancy into his words. "And so is your father. Probably. Definitely."

Arthur could not see Jojo, the blindfold utterly obscuring his view, but he could feel the tension in her grip on his arm.

He needed to be doing better. Trying harder. Attempting to meet the old man halfway.

The trouble was, there was no "almost" in marrying Mr. Bettencourt's daughter. The idea of a compromise was a pleasant one, but Arthur wasn't sure it could be achieved. And so the three of them had endured awkward teas, one terribly quiet dinner, and several afternoons of reading together in muted silence.

But at least, as Jojo had attempted to comfort him only yesterday, her father had not called him out, attempted to make him fight a duel, then killed him on the spot.

As though that was supposed to be some sort of consolation.

"You . . . you still wish to marry me, don't you?"

Arthur stopped. He felt Jojo stop beside him, heard the concern dripping from every syllable. There was a tension in her fingers on his arm that he had never felt before.

He reached blindly. Jojo immediately took his hand, intertwining her fingers with his.

"Jojo," said Arthur firmly, not caring that they were probably standing on some street with any number of people around. "Jojo, I love you. It's you I am marrying, not your father."

Her giggles made his heart contract tightly, then return to its normal rhythm.

Would he ever know how to live without her? Would the fear of losing her ever lessen?

Arthur was not sure but certainly did not wish to find out. The few weeks he was apart from Jojo had taught him swiftly that his seeming independence was worth nothing unless he had her by his side.

Everything was better with her. The sun was brighter, the leaves starting to appear on the trees greener. Birdsong was sweeter, and no challenge facing them was impossible. He needed her. He wanted her. He loved her.

"Thank you." Jojo's voice was a mere breath. "For loving me."

Arthur tightened his grip on her. "Thank you for loving *me*. All of me. As I am."

"And here I was, terrified you wouldn't love me if I weren't a duke, and this entire time—"

He had spoken his true fears at the time, difficult though it had been. Arthur was not one to reveal his emotions swiftly, but speaking so honestly to Jojo had felt natural. Necessary.

And she had proven him wrong. She loved him as he was. No title, no wealth. Her dowry would secure them a home, but Arthur had told her fiercely and frequently that the rest was to be invested to provide for their children.

His stomach lurched. *Their children. God above, his life was changing.*

"I will always love you. Just as you are," Jojo said softly, tugging on his hand to move him forward. "You are already far more noble than most of the nobility of my acquaintance."

Arthur had to laugh as they walked through what felt like a

doorway. "I am not so certain of that."

"Well, I am the expert in this matter, and you will have to trust me when I say most of the dukes I have met are absolute bores," came Jojo's teasing laugh.

It echoed strangely. Yes, they had to be inside, Arthur was almost sure. *So where on earth had she taken him—and why the secrecy?*

"Absolute bores?"

"You should have heard the Duke of Ashcott talking about his lost love," Jojo said sadly. "Oh, I do not mean the topic itself was dull. I felt rather sorry for him, in truth."

Arthur worked hard to push aside the jealousy rising by merely hearing the name of another gentleman on her lips.

She was his. This possessiveness, a desire to keep her to himself that he had not expected—would it ever fade? Would it ever change?

"Poor man," he said aloud. "I suppose he's got his title and his riches to console him."

It was not a very charitable view, but it was difficult to be charitable when a woman like Jojo had blindfolded him, led him on a wild goose chase around what felt like half of London, then led him into a mysterious place. His mind was entirely otherwise occupied.

"I suppose you wish to have a title, one day," came Jojo's teasing voice.

Arthur grinned. That was one of the greatest things about having all this out in the open with her. She had started, just in the last few days, to tease him.

Admittedly, she only did it when they were alone. But that made it all the more precious.

Arthur had no wish to change Jojo's character. Her softness and gentleness, her shyness and reserve, they were a part of her. But that was why it was so special to see this other side of her. A part of her the world never saw, that no one else shared. It was his, and his alone.

"The title of husband," he said with mock severity, "is the only title I want."

And it was taking a great deal too long to acquire, in his opinion.

"When is this wedding of ours, anyway?" Arthur added as Jojo led him a few steps farther forward. "Your father keeps telling me there's some legality he has to consider, which doesn't fill me with confidence. Are you certain he is actually going to give his permission?"

He felt the tap of remonstrance on his shoulder.

"I am just saying, I would not put it past him to object while we stood at the altar," he said darkly.

He had no true grievance against his future father-in-law. It was Mr. Bettencourt, it appeared, who had the grievance against him. As that grievance appeared to be completely based on the fact that Arthur was marrying Jojo, there wasn't much he could do about it.

"Well, you will not have to wait much longer," came Jojo's voice.

Arthur started. She was far closer that she had expected, her voice breathing into his ear as her fingers moved to the ties of the blindfold.

Hope rose. Was it possible—surely Jojo had not organized the wedding as a secret? Was he standing in a church? There was an echo here that could be like a church. Excitement rushed through him, the force of it scalding. *Oh, she was a clever one, this woman of his.* Just when he had thought it impossible that they would end the month as man and wife, she—

The blindfold fell away.

Blazing light filled Arthur's eyes and he was forced to blink for what felt like a full minute before he could see again. When his vision did return, his heart sank.

Well, they were not standing in a church.

As Arthur looked around, he could see dark paneling and a coved ceiling. It certainly had the quiet of a church, the solemnity of a church. But there were doors leading off the hallway and a few gentlemen milling about dressed in the most outrageously strange uniforms he had ever seen.

Where on earth were they?

"Jojo," Arthur said slowly.

She was beaming. Such happiness was radiating from her face that it was difficult to hold onto his suspicion. If Jojo was so pleased, then they had to be here for a pleasant purpose. But what on earth could it be?

"Where are we?" he asked.

Jojo was almost vibrating, she was so excited. "The College of Arms."

Arthur blinked. "The College of what?"

She rolled her eyes as she slipped her hand into his. "The College of Arms. It's where people come to register their coat of arms, you see?"

Misgivings were now pouring through Arthur's veins, his pulse throbbing rather painfully in his temple. The College of Arms? Coats of arms? What on earth was she thinking, bringing him to a place like this? No wonder the men here were dressed so oddly. If they discovered he was no lord, not even a gentleman, they would surely show him the door sharply.

"Jojo," Arthur hissed under his breath. "What do you think you are doing?"

But despite his tone, there did not appear to be anything he could say to lessen her joy.

Which of course, Arthur thought hurriedly, *was perfectly correct.* He wanted Jojo to be happy. Everything he did for the rest of his life would be working toward that goal.

Still. This was odd, wasn't it?

"You haven't guessed?"

Arthur shook his head slowly as they stepped to the right to avoid a gaggle of men marching forward at high speed. There was no reason why he should be here, no reason at all. Unless . . .

"Your father," Arthur said slowly.

Jojo beamed.

His heart sank. Well, he should have expected it. After all, Mr. Bettencourt had been very determined to put Arthur in his place the moment Jojo had introduced them. He should not be surprised, he supposed, that his future father-in-law had purchased a title for himself, just to make Arthur feel that much more inferior.

He pushed aside the bitterness. Well, Jojo would be a lady, if only for a few weeks until she married him. Was that enough to ensure Mr. Bettencourt—or Lord Bettencourt, as he would be—could feel superior over his future son-in-law?

"My father," Jojo said brightly. "Yes, he has pulled a few strings."

Arthur tried not to groan. "Oh, good."

Evidently his opinion was quite apparent. Jojo's face fell, and she bit her lip as she glanced at her hand, all joy fading. "You are not pleased."

This is the woman you love, that you are marrying, he reminded himself. *And though you have no family, she does. One person. Her father.*

He may not be perfect. He may have attempted to make Jojo happy in a way that had made her miserable. He may have hurt her—but it was from love. If she can see that, why can't you? *You are going to spend the rest of your life with this man in your family,* Arthur told himself firmly. Time to act more like the gentleman you pretended to be for all those months.

Time to have a little class.

"I am pleased," Arthur said, hoping the lie would become true the more he said it. "And . . . and I am happy for him. And for you."

Jojo frowned, a line puckering between her brows. "I thought you would be happy for you."

"I can be happy for me, I suppose," Arthur said, as graciously as he could manage. "It will be pleasant to be engaged to a lady, but I am sorry you will lose the distinction when you marry me."

For some incomprehensible reason, Jojo was staring as though he had lost his wits. "I beg your pardon?"

Arthur frowned in turn. It was unlike Jojo to be unclear as the etiquette of these things. She had been the one, after all, to teach him most of it.

"Once your father gets his title," he said softly, glancing about to ensure no one could be overhearing them, "you'll become a lady, won't you? But when you marry—"

"Oh, Arthur, you silly man," interrupted Jojo with a laugh.

Arthur's frown deepened. *Silly? Him?* "I don't understand—"

"Of course you don't. You've completely got the wrong end of the stick," Jojo said, her smile brilliant. "I was trying to tell you that my father has pulled a few strings—"

"Yes, you said, to gain himself—"

"To secure *you* a title," Jojo said softly.

The words echoed in his mind as Arthur attempted to untangle them. Secure him a title—him? Arthur Hebblethwaite?

No. Surely not. This was a jest.

"You tease me," he said, uncertainly.

Jojo shook her head. She was almost quivering with excitement again, all the joy that had dissipated earlier returning in full force. "You rescued me in France, you saved my life. And you returned me to my father."

Arthur opened his mouth to argue with this, hesitated, then closed it again.

One could put it that way, he supposed. Though he wasn't certain Mr. Bettencourt would have taken that view unless Jojo had given her father a very concise summary of the events that had happened.

Certain details, such as—oh, a knife held to his daughter's chest, for example. A bedding. Those probably hadn't featured in Jojo's retelling of the tale.

"Let's say for argument that I did rescue you," said Arthur, still unconvinced. "I never got the impression your father—"

"Why do you think the wedding has been delayed?" Jojo

asked softly, her expression warm. "Why do you think my father has blamed it on legal delays and difficulties?"

Arthur looked slowly about the large ancient hallway. There certainly appeared to be a great deal of paperwork moving from room to room, carried in the arms of the gentlemen here who were dressed in such ridiculous apparel.

"He . . . he was waiting for this?" he said uncertainly.

Jojo kissed him boldly on the mouth, cheeks flushing at her nerve. "You are being given a baronetcy."

"God in his—"

"You had better not curse here," she said, cutting across him quickly. "I'm not sure if they can take it away from you."

Arthur stared, then burst out laughing.

A baronetcy? Him! There had to be some mistake—but Jojo did not make mistakes. Her opinion was dependable as the sun, and as for her father . . .

"I cannot believe it," he said aloud, chest puffing with unexpected pride. "A baronetcy—surely not."

"I think you will find, Sir Arthur, that it is surely so," said Jojo, a teasing smile on her face he normally only saw in those snatched moments of privacy they were desperate to find.

Sir Arthur. Sir Arthur?

His mind was spinning, thoughts whirling through his head so rapidly, he could hardly take it all in.

A baronetcy. His future father-in-law, the staid, grumpy Mr. Bettencourt, had done all this, gone to all this effort, in recompense for saving Jojo from the French?

"It would have been quicker just to thank me," Arthur said, still partly dazed. "I—I will have a title. I will be Sir Arthur Hebblethwaite."

"And a greater baronet I have never met," Jojo said softly, though there was still mischief dancing in her eyes. "Though don't get too big for your boots, Sir Arthur."

Arthur's heart was suffused with warmth as he pulled her into his arms, his fingers interlocking at the curve of her back.

Somewhere behind him, a man gasped. "Outrageous!"

Arthur ignored him. "I will never get too big for my boots, Mrs. Hebblethwaite—"

"You're wrong there," said Jojo softly, splaying her palms against his chest, making his heart race faster.

Arthur kissed her on the forehead. "And why's that?"

Jojo giggled. "I won't be Mrs. Hebblethwaite. I'll be Lady Hebblethwaite—which I think, in truth, is what my father truly wanted."

Arthur groaned, dipping his head onto her shoulder as his future wife laughed. *Of course.* That would explain it. It wasn't truly gratitude from the man, but a determination to ensure his daughter would, by hook or by crook, become a lady.

Well, he couldn't blame him. It was a clever idea.

"Well, *Lady* Hebblethwaite," Arthur said, lifting his head and wondering how he was going to get through this conversation in the College of Arms without kissing his future wife silly. "Shall we?"

"I think we shall," said Jojo, slipping out of his embrace but only to place her hand in his arm. "I know the way."

EPILOGUE

30 March, 1811

J OJO TOOK A hasty step back. "No."

"Yes," said Arthur firmly, propelling her forward.

Though she reveled in the feeling of his hands on her buttocks pushing her back to where she had been standing, Jojo had to fight the desire to run. Run away, never to return—

"You promised me," Arthur said softly, brushing back one of her gold curls.

Jojo swallowed, nodding and wishing to goodness she hadn't. "I know I did but—"

"You said you would stand here with me, in your father's hall, and welcome all our wedding guests," said Arthur softly.

Jojo nodded again, unable to speak.

She had. She had promised him, promised Arthur she would not abandon him to face the entirety of the *ton* alone. Her father had promised her a small wedding, yet every single person in London had appeared to be in the church just an hour ago.

And now Arthur wanted her to stand here, in her wedding gown, ring newly placed on her finger, and . . . *talk to them all?*

Her stomach lurched. "I can't do it."

"Jojo—Jojo, look at me."

Jojo blinked. The haze of panic had momentarily robbed her of all sight. As she felt Arthur's warm, strong hands cupping her chin, he swam back into view. His dark eyes were serious. His hair was long, his gaze sincere.

"You vowed you would stand at my side," Arthur said softly. "To welcome everyone."

Jojo's gaze dropped as she swallowed back tears. "I know, and—"

"So if it will truly distress you," he continued, "I release you from that promise."

Jojo blinked, her gaze flickering to his once more. "You . . . you will?"

His smile was kind, his presence reassuring, and all the panic that had filled her lungs started to melt away.

"You think I would wish to force you into something you did not want to do?" Arthur asked seriously. "I would be no husband to you, my darling, if within an hour of being blessed with your hand in marriage I was making you so uncomfortable that you were close to tears."

His finger grazed her cheek.

He truly was an excellent man. One she could have spent the rest of her life looking for in the drawing rooms and ballrooms of Society, and never found.

"Y-You truly mean that?"

Arthur's gaze blazed, just for a moment. "I am not your father. I will not make you do anything you do not wish to do."

Relief, sweet relief, poured through Jojo's chest.

When Arthur had put that slim gold band on her finger, she had been certain she would never be that happy again. So far, she had been correct. The dread of the receiving line had begun building the moment they had left the church, forced to march past those numerous eyes. How could she face them? How was she supposed to—

"Jojo, listen to me," Arthur said softly, taking her by the hand and leading her away from the capacious front door propped open by a footman, and toward the drawing room.

This room was warmer. Softer. More welcoming.

Arthur shut the door behind him. "Here. We'll do it here."

Jojo's eyes widened. *Surely he could not mean—*

"Not that!" her husband added hastily. "I mean, eventually that, but I meant we can receive people here."

"Here?" Jojo repeated.

It was a most radical suggestion. Every wedding she had attended—and it was always prudent to invite the heiress, Miss Joanna Bettencourt—there had been a receiving line. It was usually outside the church, or in the hallway of the great manor house hosting the reception.

They couldn't have it here, in the drawing room!

"Impossible," she said awkwardly. "No one ever—"

"Perhaps not in your world, but in mine, there isn't a grand entrance hall to receive duchesses," said Arthur, a twinkle in his eye. "No, we do the uncouth thing of actually welcoming people from our most comfortable room. Like here."

Jojo looked around her in wonder. It was a wild thought indeed, but one she could not help but think was rather splendid.

"There you are!"

Jojo started as her father marched into the room. "Papa, I—"

"I looked for you in the hall, but you were absent. You will have to hurry," said her father swiftly. "I believe the first guest, Lady Romeril of all people, is almost—"

"We will be receiving our guests here, in the drawing room," said Arthur calmly.

Jojo stepped instinctively into the warmth and safety of her husband. Not that her father would hurt her, not in a way he comprehended. He would never lay a hand on her. He just did not understand her.

Mr. Bettencourt looked between them with thunder in his brow. "In the drawing—"

"It is what would make Joanna happy," said Arthur simply. "And so that is what we are doing."

For a terrible moment, she was certain there was to be an argument—and her father was right, she could hear Lady Romeril's voice. She must be close. If she were to overhear a disagreement between the groom and the father of the bride!

The scandal!

"I see. Good. Fine."

Jojo blinked. There was something altogether strange occurring in this moment between her husband and father. A sort of seriousness between them, a look that was most odd.

Then her father nodded. "Well, Sir Arthur, I will see to it Epwin knows—ah, Epwin!"

Jojo stared as her father walked toward the butler who had appeared tactfully by the door.

Then she let out the breath that had been painfully tight in her lungs. "Goodness."

"Yes, I shall never grow accustomed to being called Sir Arthur," her husband said ruefully.

Jojo nudged him with a laugh as a few wedding guests started to enter the drawing room curiously. "You know that isn't what I meant!"

"No, I suppose not," Arthur said, nodding to Lady Romeril who was making a beeline for them with a most determined air. "But though your father and I may have almost nothing in common, we do have one thing."

"And that is?"

"You," Arthur said wryly. "Ah, Lady Romeril. How pleasant to meet you."

It was a whirlwind. Jojo lost count of how many people she curtseyed to, how many faces she saw, how many of her father's friends muttered something about being delighted to attend, how many ladies murmured that they had never met such a charming man.

It was exhausting.

As their current conversation partner wandered off to look for some nibbles, Jojo tried hard to keep buoyancy in her voice.

"And is that all?"

"Not quite, I think," said Arthur ruefully.

Jojo sighed but managed to keep her smile intact. "Oh, good."

His glance was too knowing. "Never you fear, there's only one left. One of my guests."

She perked up. Arthur had requested invitations for only a few people, though she could not in truth recall all their names. The few she had met had been polite, quiet sort of folk. Salt of the earth, as her father would call them.

How difficult could it be to talk to one more for a few minutes?

"Ah, here he is," said Arthur, as though he was struggling not to laugh. "My dear, may I introduce to you the Duke of Chantmarle."

Jojo almost tripped over her own gown as she whirled around.

The Duke of Chantmarle? Surely not—her husband, her Arthur could not have invited such a prestigious name!

But as the tall, charming gentleman approached them, arms wide as though preparing to do the unthinkable and actually embrace her, Jojo saw it was indeed the Duke of Chantmarle. She readied herself, bracing for the unwelcome contact from a gentleman who obviously thought it was his right to embrace the bride on her wedding day.

It was therefore quite a surprise when the Duke of Chantmarle entirely bypassed her, and instead pulled Arthur into a hearty embrace.

Jojo blinked. *Arthur was friends with the Duke of Chantmarle?*

"You managed it, then!" said the duke with a dry laugh, clapping Arthur on the back. "I knew you could do it!"

When the two men eventually stepped apart, Jojo was astonished to see a slight tinge on her husband's cheeks. *Was the man embarrassed?*

"Now, I know you to actually be a duke," Jojo said nervously, lowering her voice so that their conversation would not carry across the room. "But that still does not explain—"

"Old Chantmarle gave me some rather good advice a few weeks ago," Arthur said with a grin, speaking so nonchalantly about a duke of the realm that Jojo could hardly believe it. "In a way, it is thanks to him that we are married today."

Jojo was almost certain she had heard that incorrectly. She was indebted to an actual duke for her marriage to Arthur?

No, she had to be dreaming!

"Oh, I wouldn't put it like that, though there is a modicum of truth in it," said the Duke of Chantmarle with a laugh. "I merely pointed out what a fool this cad would be if he didn't marry you, and here we are."

Jojo stared between them. "So it is you I have to thank then, for my husband's sudden and rather violent appearance at my father's door?"

She had not intended the words to be a reproof and flushed at the unintentional rudeness.

The Duke of Chantmarle, however, seemed unperturbed. "Something like that. I am pleased, naturally, to have received an invitation but even more pleased that you chose today for your wedding."

"And why is that?" asked Arthur genially.

"I'll be going up to Scotland tomorrow," said the Duke of Chantmarle, dropping his voice. "Going to root out some French sympathizers, if you must know, but keep that under your hat, old thing. Which reminds me—I must introduce you to Yates before I go up North. Do you know Yates?"

Jojo stared at the tall man in disbelief. *Surely he could not—the man was not a spy! That was simply impossible!*

Arthur appeared to be entirely calm. "No, I haven't had the pleasure. I shall miss you when you're gone from Town, of course. Perhaps you could take in a little wife hunting at the same time? I heartily recommend the married state."

"You've only been married five minutes!" exclaimed the Duke of Chantmarle as Jojo chuckled.

"Yet I already recommend it," shot back Arthur with a laugh.

Their conversation continued, but Jojo did not attempt to follow it. She was more interested in watching her husband.

It was astonishing. Just months ago, she had believed him to be the Duke of Fitzpaine. Then she had believed him to be a cad, a liar, and a deceitful blackguard. Now she called him husband.

And in each of those states, whether the Duke of Fitzpaine or Mr. Hebblethwaite or Sir Arthur Hebblethwaite, he appeared completely at ease. Able to talk to anyone, happy to hear anyone's opinions, and utterly devoted to her.

Jojo smiled as warmth flooded through her body. Her affection for him would only grow, she knew, the more she knew him. They had their whole lives ahead of them. Years.

"—mustn't monopolize the bride," the Duke of Chantmarle was saying. "My best wishes for you both."

And with a short nod of the head, he departed.

The drawing room was noisy, but thankfully their guests were all busy with their own conversations. They could, for a moment, take a breath.

Jojo leaned against her husband's shoulder. "I cannot believe that we are married."

"I cannot believe your father agreed to it."

She had to smile. "I cannot believe you are a baronet."

"Now that is something neither of us can believe," came Arthur's dry words. "I cannot believe I was able to pretend at being a duke for so long."

"I cannot believe how swiftly I was taken in," returned Jojo with a laugh, peering up at her husband. "And I cannot believe how rapid it has been, from meeting, to loving—"

"To wedding," Arthur finished, his gaze full of love. "I cannot believe you permitted me to have my way with you when you were unmarried!"

Heat flushed Jojo's cheeks, but he had spoken so low, no one else could have heard him. Those words were for her, and for her alone. The beginning of a life together that would take them along the same path, hand in hand.

"Well, I have always found," Jojo said, lifting her lips to be kissed, not caring that the whole of Society could see them, "that where there's a duke, there's a way."

About Emily E K Murdoch

If you love falling in love, then you've come to the right place.

I am a historian and writer and have a varied career to date: from examining medieval manuscripts to designing museum exhibitions, to working as a researcher for the BBC to working for the National Trust.

My books range from England 1050 to Texas 1848, and I can't wait for you to fall in love with my heroes and heroines!

Follow me on twitter and instagram @emilyekmurdoch, find me on facebook at facebook.com/theemilyekmurdoch, and read my blog at www.emilyekmurdoch.com.

www.ingramcontent.com/pod-product-compliance
Lightning Source LLC
Chambersburg PA
CBHW070346200726
48294CB00003B/802